For our 7 beautiful

Moira, Annabelle, Josephine, Mack, Michael, Lucia, and Maximilian

"Put you on the armour of God, that you may be able to stand against the snares of the devil. For our wrestling is not against flesh and blood: but against principalities and powers, against the rulers of the world of this darkness: against the spirits of wickedness in the high places. Wherefore take unto you the armour of God, that you may be able to resist in the evil day, and to stand in all things perfect. Stand, therefore, having your loins girt about with truth, and having on the breastplate of justice, And your feet shod with the preparation of the gospel of peace: In all things taking the shield of faith, wherewith you may be able to extinguish all the fiery darts of the most wicked one: And take unto you the helmet of salvation; and the sword of the spirit, (which is the word of God)."

Epistle of Saint Paul to the Ephesians, 6:11-17

Douay-Rheims Holy Bible

1

Super Safari

Book 1: The Reemergence

By: Mark and Staci McKeon

Table of Contents

Chapter 1: Lion Hunt

"You paid good money to kill a killer, Mr. Buford,"
said Mack matter-of-factly.

"Oh, boy...is that him?" the pudgy man blurted out excitedly.

"Yes, Mr. Buford, that's the lion we've been tracking." The tall man next to him lowered his binoculars slightly and couldn't help but crack a smile as his out-of-shape client continued to stammer and struggle with his hunting rifle.

"I can't believe it, Mr. O'Boyle," muttered the twitchy, sweat-drenched man as he ineptly fumbled with the shooting sticks. "The Mombasa Man-Eater..."

The lion was well over 100 yards away. Mack O'Boyle shot a nervous glance back at his client and then once again turned his attention to the dangerous quarry. "You paid good money to kill a killer, Mr. Buford," said Mack matter-of-factly. "It's what my group specializes in."

"Y-yes...right on," stuttered Buford with a strained sense of bravado. He finally managed to hoist his custom .375 H and H Magnum rifle up to his shoulder and steady it upon the platform. "It's just that I didn't think he would be so..."

"Large?" interjected Mack. "Yeah, he's a big boy. God only knows how many poor people died feeding him."

The oversize cat had not moved, but was staring straight at them both.

"He's all yours, Mr. Buford," whispered Mack. "Take him as soon as you're ready."

Sweat continued to pour off of the ruddy man's forehead. His muscles tensed and he felt like his heart was about to explode out of his heaving chest. The rifle shook as he peered though the massive scope set astride the hefty gun.

"Don't rush your shot, Mr. Buford," said Mack reassuringly. "You have time to..."

A loud blast suddenly erupted from the fat man's rifle as he simultaneously lost his footing and slid into the grass underfoot. Mack looked to see the stunned man splayed out on the ground like an upturned tortoise baking in the sun. He quickly bent down and grabbed his bewildered client in an attempt to return him to his feet.

"D-did I get him?" Buford exclaimed as he dazedly came to his senses.

"I don't know. I don't see him anywhere," murmured Mack as he nervously scanned the tall grass for the killer lion.

"Get set up again, quickly!" said Mack. A sense of urgency had entered his formerly relaxed voice and he was now on high alert. His client had obviously inflated his proficiency level with big bore rifles. All the talk back at camp about staring down cape buffalo and tracking wounded leopards was obviously complete rubbish. Given his amateurish display just now, Mack began to wonder if this man had ever hunted anything before. It was becoming more and more obvious that Clarence Buford had a big mouth and a big wallet and that was about all.

Continuing to scan for the dangerous cat, Mack tried to block out his rising anger and focus on the threat at hand. He might have a wounded lion to contend with. If that was the case, the situation for both men had just become a whole lot more dangerous.

Then suddenly, off to his right about 75 yards, Mack noticed the grass began to subtly sway. An amorphous tan shape then started to surge through the waving field, hastening towards their position. "10 o'clock, Mr. Buford. We've got company," said Mack in a low growl.

Buford was now white as a sheet. He looked pale and his knees shook as he attempted to manipulate the stout rifle once again.

"Shoot him, Mr. Buford. Take him now," said Mack as he averted his eyes for a split second to reevaluate his quivering charge.

The portly man said nothing in response. "Mr. Buford, can you do this?" asked Mack, already knowing the answer.

Clarence Buford was frozen. He didn't answer the professional hunter for several seconds. He just stood there using the shooting sticks more as a crutch than anything else. He felt faint, and the look on his face told even the most casual of observers that he would like to be anywhere else in the world right now. He was completely out of his element, and that sad truth was becoming more and more conspicuous as the seconds ticked by, the danger escalating.

"I...I don't know," he finally stammered. The bewildered man continued looking around at his surroundings like a lost child in search of his mother.

It was at that moment, as if on cue, that the incoming malevolent shape began to quicken its pace. It took only seconds for the massive cat to cover the remaining 60 yards between it and the hunters. Whether or not the lion was wounded was hard to say. The expression on the creature's face was a mixture of fanatical hate and primeval rage. Its dark visage radiated utter doom.

It seemed to the underprepared client that nothing could stop this unfolding natural disaster. Clarence Buford immediately dropped his shooting set-up and assumed a prone, fetal position on the ground. Tears mixed with hot sweat were streaming down his face and he covered his eyes as he bellowed what he believed to be his last words on Earth: "We're gonna die...we're gonn..."

The wailing man's lamentations were cut off in midsentence by the deafening roar of a .470 Nitro Express double rifle. The initial blast was quickly followed by another, and then there was absolute silence. For several moments, it seemed as if the world had stopped turning. Seconds felt like hours. Buford's quivering form continued to shake uncontrollably, but, in spite of his terror, he was able to steal a quick glance upwards. There, to his utter shock and amazement, lay the lifeless body of the cumbrous cat.

The bewildered client continued to stare straight ahead, eyes locked tightly onto the recently deceased killer. *He was still alive! But how?* The last thing he remembered was that awful devilish shape rushing towards him with its huge teeth and massive head ready to dispatch yet another human victim.

"It's ok, Mr. Buford," said a familiar voice. "Your lion is dead."

Looking upward towards the sound of the voice, disbelief slowly crept over the bloated man's face. There, directly to his left, was his guide, Mack O'Boyle. His entire left leg and half of his right were buried under the enormous cat. In his arms lay the strapping double rifle, both barrels still littered with the acrid smell of burnt gun powder.

"Now then," said Mack, in an almost matter-of-fact way, "I don't suppose you could lend me a hand with this beast. Seems he went and died right on top of me."

"What...," Buford sounded like he was choking on his words as he slowly rose and began to drink in the seemingly miraculous scene.

"What happened?" interjected Mack. "Looks like you shot him in the butt, just up from the tail. Obviously he didn't take too kindly to that."

"But he was right there. How...?" questioned the dazed man.

By now, Mack had finally processed that his client was in no position to aid him, and he set his rifle aside to pull at his right leg in an attempt to get out from beneath the behemoth specimen. "I shot him in the neck, Mr. Buford," explained Mack. "I timed his gait and aimed for his center of mass. He charged and leaped just as I let loose with my first shot, which crumpled him a bit, but he still kept coming. I let him have the second one...," Mack then motioned to the rather large, blood-soaked hole along the mid-left rib cage, "right into the boiler room, but he wasn't going to go along quietly," added the hunter as he finally pulled a bleeding right leg out from beneath the extraordinary fat cat. A great mess of claw marks could be plainly seen beneath the hunter's right knee cap.

 "Y-you're bleeding...," observed Buford as he once again found himself semi-paralyzed by the extraordinary events playing out around him.

"Yeah, nasty boy got me good. Legs are seeping a bit, but no major bleeders as far as I can tell." At this point, Mack was nearly out from beneath the lion. Both of his pant legs

8

were now soaked with blood and his shirt was torn open. Other than that, the middle-aged man really seemed no worse for the wear.

After having rested for a moment, Mack stood up, reached into his shirt, and pulled out a worn pewter medal. He gazed at the metal object respectfully, kissed it, and then replaced it inside the sullied shirt. "Yeah, just a couple of claw marks," he remarked. "I'll just add them to the collection."

Mack reached over to a day pack, opened the top, and took out a roll of gauze bandages. He then quickly got to work wrapping his legs, all the while scanning the horizon for other potential threats.

Clarence Buford initially captivated by the dead monster in front of him, now found himself in awe of the man before him. The six-foot-one-inch specimen must have been in his late fifties or even early sixties, but he had the physique of a fit thirty year old. He wore a gray beard and sported a tan bush hat. The only pieces of "jewelry" he wore were a medal of St. Hubertus and a worn pewter scapular. His blood drenched extremities were long and sinewy, and he carried multiple old scars across his arms and chest, testaments to his prior run-ins with the toothed and clawed of Africa.

"I-I'm sorry for...," Buford stopped mid-sentence. He was happy to be alive, yet the sense of shame he was now experiencing began to overwhelm him.

"You paid me to take you lion hunting, Mr. Buford," Mack interrupted. "I took you lion hunting. Now let's get a picture of you with your man-killer."

Renewed admiration overtook Clarence Buford's face. He had heard rumors about O'Boyle's hunting prowess, but never imagined that he would owe the man his life.

It was at that moment that an extended-length SUV pulled up from behind the two men. Inside were three native Africans and an elderly-looking fellow with a handlebar mustache and generous mutton chops. Once the older man emerged from the vehicle, he made his way directly towards Mack, walking past Clarence Buford as if he were not even there.

"Ahhh, it seems you've transformed another portly American hedge fund manager into the pride of East Africa!" sarcastically quipped the distinguished looking gentlemen. "I dare say, old boy," he continued as he cast a contemptible glance over at Clarence Buford having his picture taken with the immense, now lifeless cat, "not an easy task."

"I take it you saw the whole thing go down," replied Mack.

"Indeed we did," chuckled his elder. "The outcome was never really in doubt, but you really shouldn't make a habit of allowing the beasts to get so bloody close, Mack. You understand we aren't getting any younger."

"Hey, we got the cat and we got paid, Al," argued Mack. "That's really what's important at the end of the day."

A forced smile slowly cracked between Alistair Winslow's lips. "Well, I suppose there is that," he replied. "I am of the opinion that there is a whole untapped world of lucrative hunting opportunities out there for someone with your pedigree and experience. I am hearing things, Mack. Big rumors and things that..."

"The answer is no, Al," said Mack in an irritated tone.

The snappy answer set the older man back on his heels for a moment. This topic of conversation was well-trod and Alistair had had plenty of time to perfect his arguments. "But Mack, think about it, you have name recognition," rebutted Alistair. "You were the first man to successfully hunt the New Big-Five! I could contact Reginald to find out if, in fact, the rumors are true."

A cross look had formed over the blood-splattered face of the hunter. He said nothing as his companion continued to prattle on, but his body language spoke volumes.

"We are wasting our time in these backwaters, Mack." The old man's eyes narrowed as he shot a contemptible glance towards a still shell-shocked Clarence Buford. "I know you find fulfillment in this sort of work, but I am simply getting too long-in-the-tooth for such nonsense. I'm ready to..."

"Listen, Al," interrupted Mack. "I know where you are going with this. Transgenic hunting is illegal and the technology is tightly controlled. It's been that way for years. It's all underground now and there's a good reason for that. I won't get back into that life. I'm sorry you don't agree with my choices."

"No, Mack," said Alistair sadly as he stared at the ground. "It is I who should be sorry. I should not have brought it up."

Mack had finished dressing his leg wounds and attended to a rather nasty scratch across his chest. Dabbing the deepest area with antiseptic made him wince momentarily. A concerned look came over Alistair's face as he observed his best friend's obvious distress.

"It's fine, Al," Mack insisted before his friend could say anything. Al was a true confidant and sage, but sometimes he was just too motherly and over-involved. "Do we have any more work coming our way?" said Mack, eager to change the subject.

"I was contacted yesterday regarding a rogue elephant stirring up a bit of trouble in Botswana. I took the liberty of booking potential clients for a hunt."

Mack peered over at the dead lion. With the danger now passed, his client seemed supremely pleased with the impressive trophy before him. His earlier terror had all but melted away and he was at last able to revel before the dispatched nightmare beast. He exuberantly gave an enthusiastic thumbs-up to Alistair.

The Englishman could hardly conceal his eye-rolling as he turned away from the unfolding spectacle. "Oh, I'm not sure I can take much more of this, Mack. These buffoonish Americans will be the death of us all."

"They pay the bills, Al," replied Mack. "Besides, it's been awhile since we tracked elephants. That could be good sport."

"Very well," said Alistair as he turned towards the idling SUV. "Oh, by the way, word has it your son is now working with De Jaeger in Zimbabwe. It seems he has been brought in as a hunting consultant on a very significant, very secret project."

Mack said nothing for a moment. He focused on his Allen .470 Nitro Express and continued his close inspection of the stock. Mack thumbed a new, deep scratch running the length of the shiny wood. Part of the dead lion's fore-claw was buried right next to the worn recoil pad.

"I just thought you should know," added Alistair, "especially given your history with De Jaeger."

"Michael and I haven't spoken in over a year," said Mack with a sad tone in his voice. "Anyway, he's a grown man and can take care of himself," he continued, scrutinizing the dislodged claw between his thumb and index finger.

"Yes, of course he is," agreed Alistair. "Now then, it looks as though the men almost have the lion loaded. Shall we head back to camp and get you to medical?"

"I'm fine, Alistair. Nothing that a few butterfly bandages and a hot shower won't fix," said Mack.

Chapter 2: The Mega-Preserve

"The animals inside this facility are, without a doubt, the most dangerous creatures to walk the face of the earth since the time of the dinosaurs."

"Ha! You call these trophy animals?" exclaimed the burly man with a Russian accent and a jet black beard. "I kill all these animals before. I was told you have speeshal animals here. Where are all the speeshal animals?"

The man was pacing back and forth inside an ostentatious display room. He continually scanned the opulent walls. They were covered with trophy mounts from all over the world. Big cats, pachyderms, and plains game were hung one after the other. In his right hand, he carried an oversized glass of brandy, and, in his left, he was firmly clutching a large Cuban cigar. He took turns drinking and smoking as he stomped around the room like an angry, caged animal.

"Now, now Vasilli," cautioned a stout Hispanic male sporting a tan cowboy hat and a glittering golden belt buckle. "My associates have assured me that we will not be disappointed. Our host has a reputation..."

"Which precedes him, I hope!"

The short man in the cowboy hat turned his head to see a tall, good-looking, blond-haired man make his way through the grand, double oak doors. He smiled a flamboyant smile and strutted directly into the cavernous room. As he walked towards the other occupants, his face lit up even further and his forced grin doubled in size.

"Domingo!" cried the smiling man as he grasped hands with the man before him. "I'm so glad you could make it! I trust your flight was uneventful."

The man known as Domingo shot a gaudy, gold-toothed grin back to his questioner. "Nothing that a few thousand dollars couldn't remedy at the border, Bram," he said in jest.

15

"I never worry about you, old friend," returned the well-dressed Bram. He then proceeded to introduce himself to some of the other men in the room. After several minutes spent exchanging pleasantries, he glanced at his watch and quickly made an announcement. "Let's get started with tonight's informational program. Please have a seat in front of the fireplace and we will begin."

The four guests made their way to a series of heavily padded chairs in front of the towering stone fireplace and, after several seconds, were seated.

"Now then," continued their host, "for those of you who don't know me, my name is Bram de Jaeger. I'm the CEO of De Jaeger Enterprises. To my right is Dr. Josephine Fox."

Bram de Jaeger motioned to a petite young woman with light brown hair. All the men turned their attention to her and she nodded an acknowledgement, but did not smile. Her stern face was apparent and she stood as straight as an arrow, shoulders back and head held high. "Good evening. It is a pleasure to have you with us," she said in a soft, almost monotone voice.

"Dr. Fox is De Jaeger Enterprises Chief Geneticist," said De Jaeger. "She, more than anyone else involved in the Mega-Preserve project, is most responsible for the phenomenal hunting experience you're all about to enjoy."

De Jaeger then scanned the faces of the men before him. "Hunters of your caliber and means make up a very elite group. Many of you already know each other. That being said, you will be spending a significant amount of time with each other over the next several days and I believe formal introductions are in order."

With that, De Jaeger motioned to the man with the black beard. "Mr. Radovich, would you please begin?"

The large man with the Russian accent stood up in acknowledgement of his host's request. "My name is Vasilli Radovich. I am from Russia. There is not an animal in the world that I have not killed. I was told about the speeshal animals here. I have come to see for myself."

"Oh, Mr. Radovich," interjected De Jaeger, "you are most certainly in the right place...most certainly."

Next, the friendly man with the garish belt buckle stood up and smiled another of his wide gold-toothed grins. "My name is Domingo Dominguez. I am from Colombia and work in the, uh, import/export business."

Bram de Jaeger cracked a knowing smile with this bit of information. He had compiled detailed files on all of the men assembled in this room, and he knew many of them personally. Although some of his clients were engaged in legitimate business ventures, most were not. It was a well-known fact in certain circles that Domingo had been heavily involved in narcotic and methamphetamine trafficking for many decades. Rumor had it that in recent years, he had attempted to legitimize and diversify his business into pharmaceuticals and bio-tech holdings. Bram was skeptical that any significant changes in Domingo's revenue sources had really taken place. *Once a narco-terrorist, always a narco-terrorist,* he chuckled to himself.

Domingo then raised his glass and motioned towards his host. "I have hunted with Bram and his father before him and I look forward to seeing what new surprises he has in store."

17

"Thank you, Domingo," said Bram. "I guarantee that you will not be disappointed."

Next, a tall, thin, very severe-looking man stood up and addressed the group. His clothes were decidedly European and he spoke with a heavy German accent. "My name is Hendrick Gruber. I race cars, fly planes, and drive fast boats. I am here to seek a new source of adventure. It is a pleasure to make your acquaintance."

Bram graciously thanked the slender man for coming. Gruber was heavily involved in international finance. Most honest people would have labeled him as a greedy bankster. His skills at laundering money were legendary, and he had a reputation for being extremely meticulous. He was not the most experienced hunter, but he was about as cold-blooded as they come.

The man seated farthest from the rest of the group then stood, bowing towards his host and the others. He was Asian and of medium build, with black hair pulled back into a tight bun. Multiple tattoos adorned his neck and the backs of both of his hands. "My name is Matsumo Tanaka. I am from Osaka. It is pleasure to meet you."

With that, the Japanese National abruptly bowed once again, sat down, and averted his gaze, focusing on the floor. De Jaeger studied the intense looking man for an instant. Mr. Tanaka had been a late addition to the hunt. There were rumors that he had ties to the Yakuza, but Bram's people were not able to confirm this. His security check was essentially unremarkable, with no overt history of criminal activity or overt sociopathic tendencies. Given the questionable backgrounds of the other men involved in the hunt, this stood out as odd. However, Tanaka's intermediaries had shown an intense interest in the Mega-

Preserve several weeks ago and provided the money to reserve his spot after several other potential clients had failed to do so. You cannot have a hunt without hunters, and Bram had decided that this man's money was as good as anyone else's.

"Thank you, gentlemen," said De Jaeger as he addressed the eclectic group. "As most of you know, transgenic speciation was first realized 25 years ago when the genetic material from a fruit fly was combined with that of a white-footed mouse. The result was a viable, genetically unique organism capable of reproduction. It was a brave new world."

As Bram spoke, a metallic sphere emerged from the lustrous mahogany table located just in front of the looming fireplace. Bright lights emitted from the top of the device. A moment later, a collection of three-dimensional images started to take shape, oscillating back and forth before the audience.

"Transgenic technologies began to make their way into multiple industries," continued De Jaeger. "Genetically modified organisms became just another scientific reality applied to modern living and De Jaeger Enterprises was at the forefront of this scientific innovation."

An image of Bram de Jaeger as a young man and an older white-haired man was then projected up from the table. Both men were standing in front of an immense building with the De Jaeger corporate logo behind them. "My father started his company with an emphasis on transgenic bio-fuels and genetics research. Over the years, his company developed numerous patents and had production facilities all over the world. Business was good."

This image dissipated and was replaced by another: a procession of big game animals including rhinos, elephants, and big cats. "Then, 15 years ago, the 'Spizak' virus emerged on the international scene."

Bram paused for a moment as the 3-D visual display showed robust and active safari animals suddenly reduced to thin and dying creatures. The detailed depictions then changed to demonstrate vast swaths of empty African savannah. "This deadly virus decimated vertebrate species across the globe and, at one point, threatened to wipe out the majority of big game animals in Sub-Saharan Africa," he explained.

The images before the men altered to elucidate the inside of a De Jaeger Enterprises lab. Specimen tanks containing animals in various stages of fetal development were pictured throughout the massive scientific research facility. Row after row of metal tanks was each shown being inspected and operated upon by De Jaeger Enterprises scientists.

"It was chiefly through the efforts of De Jaeger Enterprises that the game species were pulled back from the brink of extinction," continued De Jaeger. "Because of our company's tireless labor, we were able to transgenetically modify new specimens that were no longer susceptible to the deleterious effects of the virus."

"The animals...they are enormous and their coloration is altered...," declared an impressed Hendrick Gruber as he stared up at the images of the transgenic species.

"Ah, yes, Herr Gruber," gushed De Jaeger, "you are most observant. The De Jaeger designed specimens were specifically engineered to be completely resistant to the effects of the Spizak virus. A select number of first generation transgenic specimens were carefully reintroduced into the wild and went on to breed with the few remaining members of that species. The subsequent offspring from those unions not only created Spizak-immune organisms, but led to a variety of phenotypic variants. Many of these new animals were larger, more resistant to injury, and, quite frankly, unafraid of human beings."

Vasilli Radovich continued to squirm and fidget in his chair. He was a man of action and was beginning to feel restless. "Mr. De Jaeger! I am hunter. I know story of transgenic animals. I have hunted transgenic animals. I was told you have speeshal animals. I am here to kill those animals!"

"Mr. Radovich has provided a beautiful segue to my final and most critical point," announced Bram de Jaeger as he quickly scanned his audience for their close attention. "Given the augmented physical characteristics of many of these early transgenics, special weapons and tactics had to be devised in order to cull specific populations after they had exceeded their environmental carrying capacity. Of course, our company was at the forefront in developing this technology. In addition to pioneering the weapons and gear used to harvest transgenics, we also developed some of the first guided hunts."

"Yes, De Jaeger," snarled Hendrick Gruber, "I am familiar with your sponsored hunts and your over-priced gear. Please explain to me why I paid you $500,000 to hunt in this particular facility."

A forced smile emerged on De Jaeger's face. Gruber's imperious attitude was grating and De Jaeger tried to ignore the German's tone. He had begun to sense a rising impatience amongst the group and decided it might be best to divert their focus for a time. "The person best suited for that task would be none other than Dr. Fox," Bram de Jaeger motioned to the scientist, "Dr. Fox, if you please."

The thin woman stepped forward and, after pressing a sequence of buttons on a handheld device, continued to stare straight ahead as the big room gradually became more and more illuminated, revealing a spacious observation area. "Gentlemen, please turn your attention to the window," said Dr. Fox. "I believe a picture is worth a thousand words."

As the hunting party stood and assembled in front of the wide viewing area, they all appeared dumbstruck by the spectacle before them. Behind the glass, as far as the eye could see, was a wild expanse of wilderness. A bulky monolithic rock structure jutted up in the middle of the enclosure. It was flanked by lush green forest, open savannah, and dark jungle environments. The landscape was dotted with numerous animals, but they were unlike anything the hunters had ever encountered.

"This, gentlemen," Dr. Fox continued, "is the Mega-Preserve: the world's first fully-contained transgenic hunting facility."

Mr. Dominguez wore a shocked expression on his face. "Th-those animals...down there in front of us...what are they?"

The young woman motioned towards the animals in question. She continued to give off an air of supreme seriousness admixed with a degree of subtle, but unmistakable haughtiness. "To the casual observer, they appear to be baboons in the genus *Papio*. However, those particular specimens contain significant amounts of DNA from *Puma concolor*, *Ursus americanus*, and *Mellivora capensis*."

Skepticism immediately overtook Gruber's stern face. "You have created a monkey with parts from a cougar, a black bear, and...a honey badger?" he asked in a tone of amazement.

Dr. Fox said nothing for a moment then replied, "Every organism inside the Mega-Preserve has a niche role to play. The animals contained within were each specially designed with the aid of a patented computer program of my own creation. There is a level of detail and orchestral design inside the Mega-Preserve that cannot be overstated. This facility houses a completely novel bio-zone which is 100 percent synthetic and fully integrated."

Hendrick Gruber began to nod his head vigorously. "Ah, yes," he said with a knowing look on his face, "that is how you are able to skirt the laws banning transgenics and their use for sport hunting. You have created a closed system. Nothing gets in or out. It is a biome within a biome."

"Actually," corrected Dr. Fox, "the Mega-Preserve is multiple biomes contained within a larger superstructure. The Preserve can be modified to extreme degrees depending on the needs of the client, from polar to sub-tropical, and most everything in between."

Bram de Jaeger now spoke up, "As for your questions regarding the legal parameters, I can assure you that De Jaeger Enterprises is 100 percent compliant with all of the conventional and transgenic hunting laws in South Africa. Our lawyers have performed an exhaustive amount of work and lobbied the appropriate groups as a means to obtain clearance for this facility. We have gone out of..."

"I care not for laws, De Jaeger. I care that the game animals inside are...how you say...challenging," impatiently interjected Vasilli Radovich.

"Challenging, yeah, you could say that." A tall, athletic man was standing behind the group with his arms folded. How long he had been there, nobody could say. He wore a leather vest and a menacing looking knife hung at his side. His face was covered in a short, well-trimmed beard. As he made his way towards Dr. Fox, his heavy cowboy boots making no perceptible footfall, yet he moved with a confident swagger.

"Who is this?" blurted out Radovich with an irritated tone.

De Jaeger stepped forward with his trademark forced smile once again on full display. "Ah, allow me to introduce Dr. Michael O'Boyle. He is this facility's head zoologist. He is also a veterinarian and accomplished hunter in his own right. He will be the lead guide on tomorrow's hunt."

"O'Boyle?" muttered Domingo Dominguez. "Where have I heard that name before?"

Michael O'Boyle's face betrayed a look of minor irritation for a split instant. "I believe you are thinking of my father, Mack O'Boyle."

"Yes, that's right," agreed Dominguez, "the transgenic killer...the pioneer."

"That's him," said Michael in a low, somewhat disdainful voice as he made his way towards the observation window and stood before the group. "We will begin the hunt at

0700," said Michael, wasting no time as he quickly sized up the men assembled before him. He had already accessed the clients' files and now mentally matched up each man with the pictures and background information that he had reviewed. "I have taken the liberty of inspecting each of your personal hunting kits and communication equipment. We will enter on foot."

"On foot?" grumbled Gruber suddenly. "Just how much walking will we be doing? I came here to hunt, not run a marathon. Do you not have some sort of conveyance?"

Bemused disgust overtook Michael's lean face for just an instant. It lasted only a moment, but it did not go undetected by most everyone in the room. It was obvious that Michael had a low tolerance for non-hunter, lazy clients, and the German man was perceived to be just that.

"Rest assured," said Michael. "We have a dedicated mag-rail system which runs throughout the Preserve. The first depot is 500 yards to the east. From there, you can access any point in the Mega-Preserve."

"And will we return here to sleep?" continued Gruber. It was becoming very clear to everyone present that the European was concerned first and foremost with his comfort. Hunting dangerous game was obviously a subsidiary pursuit.

"That option exists," explained Michael. "If you would like to save time, you can camp at several hunting chalets located inside the facility. Each is fully stocked with clothes, food, water, and hypersonic shielding."

"Hypersonic shielding? For what purpose?" It was now the mysterious Tanaka's turn to speak. By all measures, he seemed the most ill at ease of all the hunters present, appearing the least comfortable of the clients. An unceasing air of nervousness had manifested in the mystery man not long after arriving. Each new detail about the hunt seemed to generate more anxiety in him.

"The hypersonics are there for our safety, Mr. Tanaka," returned Michael. "The transgenic species we will be tracking are some of the most aggressive creatures I have ever observed. Besides their heightened physical characteristics, they all have a tendency to attack without any provocation."

The group was silent for a moment. Mr. Tanaka began to pull at his collar and fidget with his necktie as Dr. O'Boyle's words began to sink in. The others in the room also appeared somewhat taken aback by the revelation. It was only Vasilli Radovich who embraced the information as being a positive thing. "Yes, the ultimate adversary. Creatures bred for hate. They will die in most spectacular way!"

"Yes, Mr. Radovich," replied the zoologist, "they most certainly will. And it is my job and the job of the other professional hunters here to see to it that they do. Due to the nature of this kind of hunting, each of you has been fitted for 'booney-tights'. This is a mesh weave that will help reduce fatigue and monitor your vital signs."

"I am very familiar with these 'booney-tights' as you so aptly name them. It is long underwear. I do not wear such things," piped up Mr. Gruber with a rising tone of disgust in his voice.

"Yes, Mr. Gruber," replied Michael, "it is long underwear, very specialized long underwear, and I suggest you all wear it. It will allow Control to keep a close eye on each hunter and monitor all metabolic processes. If you get hurt or develop a medical emergency, the 'tights' can even initiate first aid protocols."

"Granted, gentlemen," Dr. Fox quickly interjected, "they are not everyone's idea of high fashion, but they were designed to be fully integrated with the Preserve's main operating system, Gamekeeper."

"Gamekeeper? What is that?" asked Gruber with a continued air of skepticism.

"Well, Mr. Gruber," replied Dr. Fox, "Gamekeeper is really what makes the Preserve what it is. It monitors all activity within the Preserve and helps us maintain contact with our clients. Additionally, it will ensure the perfect hunting experience by selecting specific game species and providing access points for each individual hunter."

"It sounds as if this Gamekeeper of yours is like wet-nurse to little boys," burst out Vasilli Radovich. "I was led to believe this was... how you say...free-range hunt, not turkey shoot!"

Dr. Fox appeared lost for words. She glanced over to a befuddled De Jaeger who was about to speak when he was cut off by Michael, "This is not a canned hunt, Mr. Radovich. I can assure you of that. The client's safety is always..."

It was now Michael's turn to be interrupted as Radovich suddenly stood up and began to wag a finger in the face of the young man. "Booney underwear, hypersonics, fancy computers herding animals like little sheep," retorted Radovich. "What other conclusion is one to make?"

Michael pushed his shoulders back and stared the huge Russian directly in the eye. The man with the thick black beard was several inches taller and at least 50 pounds heavier, but that did not seem to register with the smaller man.

"You need to listen to me," shot back Michael as he motioned towards the observation window. "The animals inside this facility are, without a doubt, the most dangerous creatures to walk the face of the earth since the time of the dinosaurs. It is the ultimate hunting experience for a reason. If you go inside that place thinking that you are just piddling around in some glorified kiddie park, you are going to end up dead. You may have hunted transgenics before, but you have never hunted anything like this."

At this point a very nervous De Jaeger attempted to insert himself between the two men. A tense mood had gripped the room and an obvious mutual hostility had developed between the Russian and the zoologist.

"Uh, what Dr. O'Boyle is saying," stammered De Jaeger, as he slid between the two angry men, "is simply that your health and well-being are our very highest priorities. This hunt will be a once in a lifetime experience and..."

"Bahhh," exploded Radovich holding up his empty glass, "I grow weary of this talk. I am here to kill the jumbo, nasty, speeshal animals, and drink vodka. You are out of vodka." Radovich shot one more murderous glance towards Michael. It was the look of a man who had made a lifestyle out of violence and was no stranger to the killing arts.

"Right this way, gentlemen," declared De Jaeger as he ushered the clients towards the stately wooden doors. "Dr. Fox," he continued, "would you be so kind as to escort these fine men to the dining room? We can refill your glasses there. Oh, and I am told the duck is excellent. Bon appétit!"

As Dr. Fox and the rest of the men wound their way out of the trophy room, Michael turned to follow. He had only taken a single step before he was stopped in his tracks by a firm hand on his left bicep. "Your father was never very tactful either, O'Boyle," rumbled De Jaeger. He was obviously angry and his nostrils flared as he spoke.

"Listen, Mr. De Jaeger," said Michael as he pulled his arm away from the fuming man's grip. "You hired me to lead a group of hunters on a safari inside one of the most dangerous environments ever known to man. We've barely finished beta testing and I'm certain there are still bugs in the system. Nothing manmade and this complex can be totally error free out of the box. You know I love a challenge, but you never said a thing about having clients who are known murderers, drug-dealers, sociopaths, and thieves. I mean, c'mon! Radovich? Gruber? Dominguez? Do you have to have warrants on four continents in order to be invited to this facility? It seems to me that the animals inside the Mega-Preserve have nothing on my clients!"

"The personal histories of your clients are not your concern," said De Jaeger, barely containing his rage. "You were hired for one reason and one reason only," he continued, "and that is your experience with hunting and trapping transgenics. Nothing else should concern you. Do I make myself clear?"

A forbidding moment of silence hung in the air for several seconds after the CEO finished speaking. The men's cold stares bore into each other's eyes with a scary intensity and unmistakable animosity.

"Loud and clear," replied Michael finally.

"Good," said the CEO as he spun on his heel and exited the room. "We will meet in the Control Center at 0500. See that you are not late."

"Idiot," muttered Michael as he watched De Jaeger stomp out of the room and disappear past the wood doors. Over the past several days, he found himself becoming more and more disillusioned. When he had first approached him, Bram de Jaeger had offered him a great deal of money and access to some of the most cutting-edge transgenic science Michael had ever seen. He was between jobs and had been itching to get back into the bush. It felt like the opportunity of a lifetime.

The fact that De Jaeger consorted with criminals was not unknown to Michael, but this current line-up of hunting clients was beyond notorious. Fortunately, he had dealt with men like this before. They tended to be egomaniacs and extremely selfish in their worldview. Psychopaths were difficult to deal with in the real world. God only knows how they would behave in an austere place like the Preserve where the law of the jungle had a tendency to take over.

As he touched the heavy glass observation window, a slight chill ran through Michael. He had hunted transgenics his whole life. His father taught him everything he knew. He tried to tell himself that tomorrow would just be another hunt, the same as the countless hunts he led in the past. He needed to relax and make his final checklist, but for some reason he couldn't rid himself of the feeling that the

Preserve was about to serve up some dangerous surprises that he had not anticipated. It was a premonition that he just could not shake.

Chapter 3: Murphy's Law

"I kill many animals today. I kill so many that
your people will not be able to keep up."

"I trust you all slept well," boomed De Jaeger as he inspected the group of men before him. A weird feeling of excitement mixed with dread had begun to pulse over the businessman since he had awakened this morning. His mind had been racing all night and he probably slept no more than a few hours. *Today was the day.* The Mega-Preserve had been in development for years. After many funding issues and countless other setbacks, it seemed that his dream was finally becoming a reality. Bram de Jaeger felt it was only right that he should be the one to propel the sport of transgenic hunting to its rightful place as an art form and not just some utilitarian means to an end. After all, was it not his family's company that had done so much to foster the growth and development of this type of hunting? Now, he and his organization would show the world, yet again, why the name De Jaeger was synonymous with hunter.

Each of the clients had been fully outfitted with the most up-to-date technology and weaponry available. For his part, Radovich looked like a man prepared to invade a small country. He whistled cheerfully while he busily inspected his massive jet black hunting rifle chambered in .600 Overkill. It was obvious to the others in the group that he was by far the most experienced of the men.

"Speeshal hippo, lion, and elephant, De Jaeger," quipped the hulking Russian with a macabre sing-song voice. "That is what I expect to see today. I kill them and eat them."

"Oh, most assuredly, Mr. Radovich," responded De Jaeger nervously as he closely watched the smiling Russian psychopath. "Your designated prey species have all been uploaded into Gamekeeper. Once the hunt begins, you will each be directed to the appropriate habitat within the 32 sectors which make up the Mega-Preserve. Dr. O'Boyle and his staff will be there to assist you. We can guarantee 100 percent opportunity. The rest is up to you."

"I am still not certain how you can make such statements," said Gruber as he fastened a small backpack around his thin shoulders. "I have never encountered anyplace in the world in which the opportunity to see game was 100 percent. I remain skeptical."

Radovich had voiced similar concerns last evening at dinner. He now shrugged his shoulders at the question and busied himself with a final gear check, commencing his peculiar singing.

"I won't bore you with all the details, gentlemen," responded De Jaeger in his most fake sincere voice. "Additionally, the Preserve has a multitude of proprietary secrets which must be maintained in order to assure the exclusivity of our brand."

"Who cares?" piped up Dominguez as he slung his scoped rifle over his shoulder. "I came here to hunt, drink, and get away from mi esposa. I say we get to it!"

"Ah, yes, gentlemen!" exclaimed De Jaeger. "The game is afoot! Now then, please grab your gear and meet up with Dr. O'Boyle and his team.   I will be in the control room monitoring each of you. Happy hunting!"

With that, De Jaeger turned to leave. As he did, he shot a cautious glance at Michael O'Boyle. The two men said nothing, but a renewed sense of mutual animosity continued to make itself known. Tension between them had been building for weeks. The Preserve was a tremendous financial undertaking and a great deal was now riding on the success of this inaugural hunt. De Jaeger had spoken openly about his "investors" and their very keen interest in his operation. He had made it a habit of reminding Michael and the other employees almost daily about the supreme importance of today's big event.

Focusing on his clients and staff, Michael quickly noted that everyone on his team was present and accounted for. Each client had been assigned a Professional Hunter, or PH, to accompany and specifically guide them. Each of the PHs had been hand-picked by Michael himself. He knew all of the men personally and had a good working relationship with each of them.

"Alright, please listen up," announced Michael. "We will be getting started in a few minutes and I want to go over a few final details." Everyone in the room stopped speaking and turned their attention to Michael. Even Radovich stopped what he was doing and looked up at the young man.

"Gamekeeper will monitor your location and keep me and the rest of the guide staff apprised of how each of you are doing. Your PH will be with you at all times, so you will never be completely alone. If you get hurt or lost, stay in that sector, and we will come to get you."

"Once we kill an animal, what happens then?" asked Tanaka as he fingered a rather funny looking knife on his belt. "Do you expect us to, uh, process the animals?"

Michael could not help but chuckle. Of all the men here, this Mr. Tanaka gave the impression of being the most out of his element. Even to the casual observer, it would be obvious that this man really had no clue as to what he was doing. *Why was he here? How had he learned about the Mega-Preserve?*

"Oh, no, Mr. Tanaka," replied Michael as he stifled a grin. "You kill the animal and my staff will haul it and skin it for you. The idea is that you get to keep hunting as much as possible. We take care of the mundane tasks."

Tanaka customarily bowed and said nothing. He continued to nervously play with the jeweled knife at his waist and scanned the room with a look of trepidation. Michael made a mental note to keep an extra pair of eyes on him. It was readily apparent he had no business being here and his presence could be a major liability.

Radovich had already started for the oversize metal double doors leading to the habitat boundary. Confidently, he hoisted the obnoxiously oversized .600 Overkill onto his shoulder and smiled.

"I kill many animals today. I kill so many that your people will not be able to keep up. They will want to quit. Yes, this is what I will do. Open big door so I can kill speeshal animals!"

As if on cue, the mammoth metal doors separating the ready room from the Preserve began to grind apart. Radovich was the first to make his way through, aggressively stomping forward into the bush, and his PH, Jonathan, a short, thin man from Zimbabwe, ran to catch up. Within seconds, the sound of gunfire erupted.

"Ah, it has begun! First kill goes to Radovich," announced De Jaeger with glee as he glanced at his tablet's data screen, "A transgenic sable. Control, route the game processors."

Turning to the rest of the group, Michael smiled and said, "You fellas better get a move-on. That Russian seems bent on getting all the animals for himself!"

Without a word, the remaining hunters began to file out of the staging room. Matsumo Tanaka followed last in line. He appeared terrified as he clung to his rifle like a child holding onto a security blanket. His PH, an old Afrikaans farmer named Wulf, just shook his head with a look of disdain as he accompanied the man forward. He obviously felt as though he had drawn the short straw, and, given what he had seen so far, Michael could not argue.

As the last of the men stepped out into the Preserve with their assigned PHs, Michael turned to De Jaeger. "Well begun is half done, Mr. De Jaeger. It looks like Radovich has kicked things off nicely," said Michael, trying his best to be pleasant.

De Jaeger turned only slightly, and once again struggled to produce his best forced smile, but could only muster a half-hearted sneer. "I'm not at all worried about the Mega-Preserve, Dr. O'Boyle," replied De Jaeger snidely. "The technology is beyond solid, regardless of your unfounded worries surrounding my project. Your job is to see to it that the human factor is controlled." With that, Bram turned brusquely, not waiting for a reply, and proceeded to the elevator. He was feeling very positive right now, and a miscreant like Michael O'Boyle was not going to ruin the mood.

As the doors to the elevator closed, he shot a final glance at Michael. The young man had already loaded his gear and was headed out the grand bay doors. Watching him, Bram couldn't help but think about just how much the man looked like his father, Mack. It had been many years since the two men had spoken. Suffice to say, they had not parted on good terms.

Pretentious jerk, thought Bram. *Like father, like son*, the CEO mused as the elevator doors closed. While he pressed a series of buttons on the wall of the elevator, his mind wandered back to his youth and his first meeting with the elder O'Boyle. The old man and his son both shared a penchant for being insubordinate know-it-alls. He would need to seriously consider replacing O'Boyle at his earliest convenience. A sudden feeling of elation took hold of Bram as he imagined sacking the zoologist. He would revel in it, but for the time being he would have to be content monitoring the hunt from Control and leaving the dangerous scut work to his underlings.

The lift then began to slow and the elevator doors slid open, at which time De Jaeger found himself looking directly at Dr. Fox. "Good morning, Mr. De Jaeger," said Dr. Fox in her soft, serious voice. "The hunt appears to be going well so far. As expected, Radovich has gotten off to a quick start."

An array of view screens linked to surveillance cameras lined the walls of the control room. A separate bank of monitors contained the biophysical profile for each member of the hunting party.

"Three animals in 20 minutes, and his heart rate is in the 60s?" remarked Dr. Fox.

"He's a natural born killer, Dr. Fox," De Jaeger smirked. "Oh," he added, "if you think he's scary, I've heard his older brother is even worse."

A look of abject repulsion snuck onto the geneticist's face. "Uhh...," was all she could muster to say.

"Let's just say that the information in his INTERPOL file would be enough to keep the most hardened criminal awake at night." As he said this, the surveillance camera zoomed in on Vasilli Radovich's face. Dr. Fox physically recoiled at the sight of the bulky Russian's grim visage. His beard and forehead were a blood-smattered mess and his face seemed contorted into an unholy combination of unhinged delight and fanatical intensity.

"Oh," added De Jaeger jokingly, "did I mention Vasilli is also single?"

Dr. Fox said nothing and only shook her head as she continued to scan the monitors for the other clients. Mr. Dominguez just bagged a nice transgenic warthog and Mr. Gruber was stalking a majestic, atypical kudu. Both men seemed to be enjoying the experience thus far.

"Where is Tanaka-San, I wonder?" muttered Fox with serious apprehension on her face. She had also taken notice of the Japanese man's weird demeanor. He had the appearance of being so ill at ease last evening and again today while preparing to leave for the hunt. Even she, a non-hunter, could tell that he really had no business taking part. "He appears to have left the main group and is headed north, towards Sector 31."

"What do you mean?" said De Jaeger as he took a sip of coffee. "Isn't he on camera?"

"No, his biophysical profile was up just a moment ago, but the feed's been cut."

De Jaeger's easy attitude suddenly turned scared.

"The feed's been cut?" he uttered with serious concern. "What do you mean? We have backup systems. You told me that with Gamekeeper we would be eyes on at all times."

A flushed redness crept onto the scientist's thin face. Yes, Gamekeeper was designed to trouble-shoot these problems before they started. Fox and her team had designed the system from the ground up. It was supposed to be perfect.

Suddenly, a resounding rumble could be felt in the distance. In an instant, the entire control room was cast into pitch darkness.

"Dr. Fox," whined Bram de Jaeger, "what's happening?"

"I-I don't know," sputtered Fox. "Backup diesel generators should kick on..."

As if on cue, the lights in the control facility suddenly whirred back to life. Dr. Fox scanned the computer screens with much expectation, but the monitors remained a somber black.

"Gamekeeper is off-line," she said, her voice breaking. "I can't communicate with it at all."

"Do you know what is going on inside the Mega-Preserve?" queried De Jaeger in a scared voice. "What's happening with the clients? Can you reach O'Boyle?"

"No," she replied. "Radovich, Dominguez, Tanaka, Gruber, O'Boyle, the PHs...all the feeds are down. It won't respond."

"Won't respond?" screamed De Jaeger. "You told me this could never happen! You told me that this supercomputer of yours was beyond reproach. Do you have any idea what will happen to us if those men are hurt, say nothing about killed, inside our facility?"

Dr. Fox could say nothing. Tears began to gather at the corner of her eyes and she could feel her entire body begin to tense up. This unfolding nightmare was just that, a bad dream, and she wanted to wake up and reset the day in the worst way. "Mr. De Jaeger," she pleaded. "I will find a way to reestablish contact with the team. O'Boyle's PHs are well-trained. We have rehearsed and trained for contingencies. Michael will..."

A lone monitor suddenly lit up on the other side of the room. After a few seconds, a string of foreign-looking computer codes began to display itself on the screen. De Jaeger and Fox both ran to the solitary device and peered at it for several anxious minutes.

"You mind telling me what your computer is saying?" Bram half-yelled at her.

Dr. Fox studied the code series for several more seconds and said nothing. Shocked incredulity began to take over her face, but she could manage no words. Her mouth simply dropped open, seemingly frozen.

"Dr. Fox? Hello?" said De Jaeger in a singularly patronizing tone. "What's going on? Is Gamekeeper getting its house in order or not?"

Dr. Fox shook her head slowly. What she was reading could not be real. It was impossible, but then again, how else could she explain not only Gamekeeper's catastrophic failure, but also its complete inability to come back online and reestablish control of the Mega-Preserve.

"Well, Dr. Fox, what's our status?!" De Jaeger had long since reached his breaking point. He was no longer even trying to hold it together.

Fox turned towards De Jaeger, took a deep breath, and did her best to compose herself. "The good news is that Gamekeeper is back online."

A puzzled expression leapt onto Bram's face. *If Gamekeeper was working, why hadn't full power been restored? Why were all the feeds still dead? Why hadn't the auto diagnostics given a full account of what had happened?*

"G-good news?" stuttered De Jaeger. "What are you saying?"

Fox let out a deep sigh, "Gamekeeper is...ignoring me. This is not my code," she said, pointing to the monitor.

"Ignoring you?" sputtered De Jaeger. "If it's not your code, whose is it?"

"I have no idea," she replied with a shrug of her shoulders. "I did not write any of this," she said with a defeated tone in her voice. "The only thing I can say is that Gamekeeper is no longer under my, er...our control, and...," Dr. Fox's stilted speech suddenly halted. She continued to glance back and forth from the monitor to De Jaeger. The meager light emitted from the computer screen made her face look gaunt and drained of vitality.

"Spit it out, Fox!" screamed De Jaeger. "C'mon!"

Pushing her glasses up her nose, Dr. Fox hesitatingly turned towards her employer. "Gamekeeper has somehow inverted its programming, Mr. De Jaeger. The program parameters I wrote have been deleted or buried. The entire facility has been co-opted and I cannot attest to the safety of anyone inside the Preserve at this moment."

"Inverted its programming...," muttered De Jaeger. "What in the world does that even mean?"

Dr. Fox looked up at Bram with a pained expression. It was a look of combined terror and strange bewilderment, and the scientist struggled to find her voice.

Finally, she spoke. "Well, it means that every person in the Mega-Preserve is in mortal danger. It signifies that the transgenic animals are no longer the quarry; the hunters are."

Chapter 4: Bad News

"He was a dangerous rogue, Al.
He needed to be put down."

The old bull elephant was massive. His assertive bleach-white tusks swayed back and forth as he eyed the hunting party before him. The group had been doggedly tracking the huge animal for two days. It had left a horrible path of destruction in its wake. Multiple fields had been destroyed and several farmers killed. The elephant had become a major public safety hazard and that was why Mack and his men were here. Sensing the impending danger, which this new group of humans posed, the big bull let out a loud trumpet and charged immediately towards Mack's position.

"Here he comes, boys," announced Mack in a surprisingly calm tone. "Spread out!"

Alistair had not had time to line up another client for this particular hunt. After the Mombasa hunt, Mack was more than happy to take a break from his duties as a professional hunting guide. His chest and leg still smarted from the lion and he could tell he was not at 100 percent.

The team urgently scattered from the path of the charging monster, but the elephant made an abrupt right hand turn and ran straight towards Mack. The old beast held a crazed look in its eyes as it continued to bear down directly on his position. In some preternatural way, it seemed as if Mack's massive quarry had determined that the old hunter was chiefly responsible for orchestrating the unrelenting pursuit, and this headlong attack was a final desperate attempt to turn the tables on its dogged opponent.

The enraged elephant let loose with another loud trumpet that was suddenly punctuated by the sound of a double rifle. One thunderous shot rang out, followed by another. The once defiant beast crumpled unceremoniously into a tremendous pile of skin and muscle, never to move again.

"I say! Stupendous shooting, old boy...stupendous!" yelled Alistair as he peered out from behind a moderate-sized baobab tree.

"That reminds me of the old days, it does. The brute never stood a chance." The old Englishman made his way over to the newly lifeless animal and carefully inspected the remarkable wounds along its forehead.

"Excellent grouping, Mack. I rather like the symmetry," continued Alistair as he probed the newly formed holes with his finger. Even after all these years, the old hunter was fascinated by the mechanics of the hunt and made it a point to conduct a limited necropsy on any kill he encountered.

Mack had watched this display many times. He understood Alistair's morbid curiosity, but participating in the post-hunt ritual no longer held any interest for Mack. "He was a dangerous rogue, Al. He needed to be put down."

Upon hearing that statement, Alistair turned his attention away from the dead pachyderm and towards his long-time friend. A look of pity mixed with bewilderment appeared on his face and he couldn't help but shake his head ever so slightly. "You really have lost the fire, lad," he said forlornly. "The thrill you used to get hunting these dangerous beasts has all but vanished."

Mack busied himself with inspecting his ammo belt and cleaning his gun. He did not even bother looking up at his friend as he began to speak. "It's just a job," Mack said softly. "That's all it ever really was. The fact that you continue to romanticize it, well, that's your own business. We kill for money. It's as simple as that."

Alistair stood in stunned silence for a moment, unsure what to say. Finally, he spoke. "I'm truly sorry about what happened between you and Michael, but why stifle the one thing that has always brought you pleasure?"

Mack set down his hefty double rifle and looked Alistair in the eyes. "Michael was...is right," replied Mack as his voice broke slightly. "I was a terrible father and a selfish jerk. I spent the majority of my adult life in the bush and what do I have to show for it? Trophies? Hunting records? Even when Mary was diagnosed with pancreatic cancer, I still couldn't be bothered. The caribou were migrating and the hunting was supposed to be superb that year. My priorities were so screwed up. They probably still are." Mack's voice trailed off as he turned slightly and stared out into the African bush.

Both men said nothing more for a moment. The rest of Mack's entourage busied themselves with processing the freshly killed elephant. The normal chatter that accompanied such an event was strangely muted. The tense interaction between the two men had not gone unnoticed by everyone, and those in the immediate area fell into a deep silence. Mack's personal life was a topic that never came up. It was rumored that he had experienced a falling out with his son some years ago, but the details were never made public.

"Well, then," finally piped up Alistair, "I believe it is even more crucial that I tell you what was relayed to me this morning. It seems Michael, along with his team of hunters and four clients, has gone missing. He was overseeing the opening of a new De Jaeger hunting facility when the computer system was...corrupted."

Upon hearing this, Mack shook his head and tightly gritted his teeth. "What do you mean, 'corrupted'?"

Alistair shrugged his boney shoulders earnestly. "Nobody really knows," he admitted. "De Jaeger's tech people have been working 'round the clock to reestablish control. As of this morning, they still had not heard a word from the people inside."

Mack's face was red and his eyes became narrowed slits. "What was he thinking working for a scum bag like Bram de Jaeger? You can't trust those creeps. His old man was an international criminal. I told Michael they were all bad news."

"Yes, the De Jaeger name is one of infamy. Why I remember when Hans Botha and I met with De Jaeger...," began Alistair.

"They have to have a contingency plan, Al," interrupted Mack impatiently. "Who's been tapped to perform the extraction?"

"Well," said Alistair, "the details are sketchy, but it sounds like Arvid Russell and his team was called in."

A momentary sign of hope emerged on Mack's face. Arvid Russell was a former Recce Commando. He was a combat veteran and now specialized as a military contractor. In recent years, he and his team had worked providing executive protection to high-profile clients in and out of Africa and the Middle East. Arvid also liked to hunt, and he and Mack had become friends.

"Russell's good," replied Mack. "His team is very experienced."

"They most certainly are," responded Alistair, "but they also have not been heard from since they made ingress into the hunting environment."

Mack found himself shaking his head unconsciously. There had to be some mistake. Alistair's contacts must have bad intelligence about De Jaeger's project. "You're saying the entire team has gone missing?" said Mack incredulously. "What is going on in there?"

Alistair once again shrugged and shook his head. "Nobody really seems to know. It's all very hush, hush. Rumors have been swirling for some time, but all we really know is that some influential money clients were recently flown in for a very special hunt."

Mack looked pensive for a moment. If De Jaeger was involved, the whole operation was shady at best. "What are we talking about, Al? Heavily modified transgenics? 2nd generations?"

Alistair was visibly bothered by the fact that he did not know more and could share only the most general details. He prided himself in knowing all of the information about a topic. He was a researcher and traded in information since he no longer actively hunted. "I'm sorry, Mack, but nobody can say for sure. I do know that De Jaeger did away with most of his genetics staff about two years ago after he hired a woman by the name of Fox. Up until a short time ago, nobody had really heard of her. Now, she's one of the most sought after genetic designers in the industry."

Mack thought for a few moments. *Fox?* He reflected on the time when he met a woman named Dr. Josephine Fox about 8 years ago in Siberia. At that time, she was working with the Russian government regarding transgenic technologies and their possible applications to help with Asiatic big cat conservation efforts. "I've met her, Al," said Mack. "Smart lady, but really weird."

"Yes, well...uh," continued Alistair, "My sources tell me that Fox had some revolutionary transgenic designs she was getting set to unveil. Supposedly, these were radical upgrades and modifications far exceeding anything we have seen in existing transgenic biotechnologies."

"That's just swell," snorted Mack. "My son could be going toe to toe with this crazy woman's version of Godzilla for all we know."

Alistair nodded his head in sad agreement.

"What about Michael's hunting clients? What do we know about them?" asked Mack.

"Hmmm," mumbled Alistair as he searched his recollection for any information he might have gleaned regarding the identities of the De Jaeger clients. "Well, that is a guarded secret and is supposed to be confidential, but I do know that the list includes Vasilli Radovich and Hendrick Gruber, both of whom were recently spotted in Pretoria. They received armed escorts and were observed leaving the city not long after arriving."

"Oh, this just gets better and better!" shouted Mack. "The Russian psycho and the German bankster creep. Who better to have on a hunt?"

"If you don't mind my saying, Mack," interjected Alistair, "I am most certain your son knows exactly what and who he is dealing with. He's out to prove something to himself. Whatever De Jaeger and this mad scientist of his have created, it's big and it's bold. Bram needed the best hunter in the world to oversee whatever it is he's cooked up. He hired your son. Really, he is more like you than either one of you would ever like to admit."

Mack had busied himself with a variety of clean up tasks as Alistair continued talking. He placed his double rifle inside its case and quickly began making his way towards the waiting SUV. "Awwh, stop the psychobabble and just get things tied up here," Mack snapped at his friend.

"Where are you going?" asked Alistair with a look of keen knowing already spreading across his aged face.

"I'm headed to Pretoria," said Mack in a matter-of-fact tone, "and then I'm going to get my son."

A huge smile broke out beneath Alistair's droopy mustache. "And how do you plan on getting there, pray tell?"

"I don't know, Al," shrugged Mack. "I'll have to arrange a plane when I get to the airport."

"No need to, old boy," smiled Alistair. "Reginald has already made arrangements. You leave in an hour."

Upon hearing this, Mack just smiled. The old Brit really did know him better than he knew himself. Alistair was a fantastic friend and a wonderful business partner. In spite of their very real philosophical differences, he could always count on Alistair to be operating several steps ahead.

"Thanks, Al."

"No need to thank me," said Alistair, his voice cracking slightly. "Just get your son back in one piece. Godspeed, old boy!"

With that, Mack threw the SUV into gear and barreled down the road with a flurry of African dust and dirt in his wake.

Chapter 5: The Coming of Vladimir

"…'a brilliant woman' was going to create a 'super safari' for him to hunt in. It looks to me as if you have failed…and failed very badly."

"I need to know what's happening inside there!" screamed Bram de Jaeger as he waved his arms wildly. "It's been 36 hours since we heard anything from O'Boyle and his people. Now Russell's team is out of communication, too?"

Dr. Fox was clearly exhausted. Nothing in her career as a researcher and scientist had ever prepared her for this. She continued to search her mind for a solution, some means to regain control, and break the chaotic spiraling. Nothing was working.

Arvid Russell and his group had not been heard from for over 12 hours. When they had first arrived at the Mega-Preserve installation, the team, along with its leader, gave off an air of supreme confidence. Even after she briefed the operators with a detailed situational report, they had all seemed brazenly disinterested. To them, this remained a recovery operation with a few fancy safari animals thrown in for good measure. Russell even went so far as to say he expected his team would have the hunting party back, safe and sound, in time for dinner.

Well, if this was supposed to be an easy rescue operation, I'd hate to see what a difficult one entails, Fox thought to herself.

Bram de Jaeger had become increasingly unhinged as the hours ticked by. Arvid's crew was his best hope after all other interventions had failed. Even now, his IT people had made no progress getting on top of the problem. After a day of missteps and false hope, De Jaeger was looking for a miracle. "Arrrgh, the men inside the Preserve...," De Jaeger paused for a moment.

"Yes?" replied Dr. Fox, unsure what Bram was trying to say.

"The clients inside there...those men have associates...people they work with," explained De Jaeger as he pointed wildly towards the now dark observation window. "I don't need to remind you how poorly those men will take this information."

"I can tell you personally that they will not take this information well, not well at all." The booming voice came from the back of the darkly lit control room. It belonged to a black-bearded, towering man dressed in a dark leather jacket. His bull-like neck was adorned with a multitude of thick, gold chains intermixed with Russian gangster tattoos. He clutched a large cigar in his right hand, the smoke of which encircled his grandiose frame as it wafted upwards. To his left and right appeared an intimidating cadre of gun-toting men with stone faces and emotionless, dead eyes.

An already frazzled Bram de Jaeger let out an audible gasp as he stared up at the angry looking man and his intimidating entourage. "Who are you?" stammered De Jaeger. "How did you get in here?"

The striking man methodically began to take off his jacket and then proceeded to roll up his sleeves as if he were preparing for some sort of heavy activity. "I walked in through the front door," explained the bearded man with a matter-of-fact tone, "right past that pitiful bunch of skinny dogs you call your security team."

As he spoke, he stepped closer to De Jaeger and Fox, overwhelming them. There was something very familiar about the man's demeanor, but De Jaeger's nerves continued to be so rattled that he found it more and more difficult to process all that was happening around him.

"As for whom I am...," continued the man as he carefully caressed the hilt of a menacing knife hanging from his hip, "my name is Vladimir Radovich. Vasilli is my younger brother. I have come to this disgusting backwater to take him home and kill the incompetent fools who have put his life in danger."

Both Fox and De Jaeger were speechless. This man had just promised to kill them both and by the looks of things, he seemed more than suited to the task. After several seconds of shocked silence, Bram found his voice. "Whoa, whoa," he pleaded, "let's just slow down here a minute. Your brother knew the risks associ..."

Vladimir did not wait for De Jaeger to finish speaking. He firmly took hold of his gigantic knife and began to draw it out. "Nyet!" Vladimir screamed at De Jaeger as the once proud entrepreneur found himself hurriedly backpedaling into a dark corner. "You are a coward and a weakling. Vasilli was stupid man to associate himself with likes of you. It is just like Vasilli - too much hunting and not enough thinking. I kill you now, dog."

Continuing to bear down on the cowering De Jaeger, Vladimir Radovich single-mindedly attempted to make good on his deadly threat. The tense moment was suddenly interrupted as a tall, bearded man stepped into the room and held up his hands. "Stop!" called out the stranger as Vladimir's security team scrambled to address the new player. "Don't kill him," the stranger continued as the Russian's men forcefully pushed him up against the wall and began to search him. "At least not until I get some answers!"

Vladimir Radovich was within inches of Bram's face and he could feel the ominous Russian's cigar-tainted breath on his forehead. He was feeling sick to his stomach and his legs started to shake uncontrollably. Upon hearing the man's voice, De Jaeger's head shot up with a bewildered look in his eyes. "M-Mack!" he sputtered with a mix of fear and hope.

"Been a while, Bram," replied Mack. "I have to say you've looked a whole lot better. Where's Michael?"

De Jaeger said nothing in response to the question. His mind was overtaxed, full of frenetic thoughts. Mack's arrival had served as a stay of execution for him. If he could just keep Vladimir and Mack busy, maybe he could make his way out of this situation alive.

With no warning, the head of Vladimir's security detail roughly grabbed Mack by the arm, briskly searched him, and shoved him towards the middle of the control room. Then he hurriedly crossed the floor and handed Vladimir an attractive Bowie knife with a whitetail deer antler handle. Speaking in Russian, he explained to his boss that the knife was all they had found on the new arrival. Vladimir nodded and admired Mack's robust Bowie knife. "Custom work...very nice," he noticed as he inspected the handle and exposed the sheathed blade. "Who are you?"

De Jaeger managed to stand up. Several of Vladimir's men had their guns trained on the CEO as he attempted to compose himself. "M-Mr. Radovich," De Jaeger managed to spit out. "Please allow me to introduce Mack O'Boyle, the most decorated hunter in modern history...a living legend in the..."

Vladimir spun around and with a venomous hiss, screamed, "Quiet, De Jaeger! I care not for your silly... how you say... appellations. I am here for my brother.

Does this man know where he is?" Vladimir stared intently at Mack as he turned his attention back towards the hunter.

"I'm here for my son," replied Mack.

"Your son is amongst the hunting party, then?" queried Vladimir as he took a step closer to Mack.

"Well, yeah, you could say that," responded Mack. "It's my understanding that he's leading it. Isn't that right, Bram?"

Everyone's focus was trained upon the head of De Jaeger Enterprises. "Yes," Bram answered, his voice quavering a bit. "Dr. O'Boyle and his team are leading four clients, your brother included, inside the Mega-Preserve."

"Hmm," said Vladimir as he thought for a moment. "I care not for your son, old man. If he had done his job, my brother would be safe and I would not need to be here!"

Radovich then turned towards De Jaeger, once again fingering the exotic knife at his hip. "Now then, tell me where my brother is and I may cut off only your arms."

"I-I'm afraid it is not that easy, Mr. Radovich." Dr. Fox said weakly as she looked over at the murderous man and attempted to find her voice in the midst of the frightening situation. She had never been so terrified in all her life, but Mack O'Boyle's arrival had given her a chance to minimally compose herself. "W-we've already sent in an extraction team, a group of military contractors," she explained. "W-we've lost all communication with them."

"And who might you be?" growled Vladimir as he stared at the diminutive scientist.

"D-Dr. Josephine Fox," she responded. "I'm this facility's lead geneticist."

"So, you work for the sniveling cur?" Vladimir said as he motioned over his shoulder at De Jaeger.

"Y-yes, I do," she admitted.

"Ahh, so you are the one who made this glorified petting zoo, eh?"

Dr. Fox said nothing. As scared as she was, Josephine was still very proud of what she had helped create. The Mega-Preserve was her greatest professional accomplishment to date and a part of her really resented Radovich's demeaning remarks.

"Vasilli knew all about you," continued Vladimir. "He told me that 'a brilliant woman' was going to create a 'super safari' for him to hunt in. It looks to me as if you have failed...and failed very badly."

"We still don't know exactly what has happened, Mr. Radovich," explained Fox. "I am certain if we can just..."

"Nyet!" interrupted Radovich in his now customarily savage manner. "It has been too long. You know this. You create pathetic menagerie of pretty animals whose sole purpose in life is to die in spectacular fashion. Vasilli has killed everything worth killing on this planet at least twice. He is most capable hunter I know. Yet, he comes to your stupid little zoo and he is lost inside? How can this be?"

"I'm sorry," responded Fox, "We just don't know. We are on emergency backup generators and the video feeds are all down. The facility's regulatory program is no longer responding. It has begun to act...," Dr. Fox paused in mid-

59

sentence, unsure if she should continue with her explanation. She quickly scanned Bram de Jaeger's face for some guidance. Bram just stared back at his employee with eyes wide open, appearing just as tentative about exposing all the details regarding Gamekeeper's cooptation.

"It has begun to what?" snapped Radovich. The nonverbal communication between Fox and De Jaeger had not escaped him. It was becoming more and more obvious to him that Vasilli had received only the barest amount of information regarding the inner working of the Mega-Preserve. Something very weird had obviously happened in this place and Vladimir Radovich was intent on finding out just what it was.

"What Dr. Fox means to say is that the regulatory system, a program we call Gamekeeper, has developed a few minor glitches. It is really nothing that we cannot handle. If we just had a few more hours, I am sure..."

"That's a load of garbage and you know it," interrupted Mack from across the room. Radovich's security forces still held him at bay, but in spite of this, the hunter remained calm and collected. "What these two are really saying is that everything out there has become one gargantuan unknown." Mack motioned to the still blackened, plexiglass observation window along the front of the room. "This whole twisted enterprise has gone from weird to outright belly-up," he continued. "Fox and De Jaeger haven't got a clue about what's happening inside. Due to the loss of power and/or this Gamekeeper thing going rogue, the system's safeguards are all offline. Russell's team is probably dead. I'm guessing every transgenic organism in there has been set loose or will be. The place has become a biological death trap."

"I would have to say that is a gross misrepresentation of the present situation," stammered De Jaeger. "We don't know any of that for sure. We have..."

"...lost control of your super computer, lost contact with your rich, connected clients, lost contact with the extraction team sent to find them, and lost contact with my son, Bram," interjected Mack. "So, yes, I think my assessment of the situation is spot on."

"You seem to know a good deal about this place," perceived Vladimir as he motioned for his men to release Mack.

"Yeah, Bram and I have a history," replied Mack as he made his way towards the sole functioning computer screen in the control room. Mack reached into his front lapel pocket, produced a pair of worn bifocals, and carefully set them astride his weathered face. After several seconds of reviewing the data on the screen and then perusing Dr. Fox's notes, Mack looked up with a disgusted frown on his face.

"Well, looks like you and the doctor here did it, Bram," quipped Mack as he folded his bifocals and carefully replaced them back into his front pocket.

"Did what?" Radovich countered. "What do you mean?"

"You want to explain, or should I?" replied Mack.

It was quite obvious to all present in the room that Dr. Fox was not at all interested in speaking on the topic she feared Mr. O'Boyle was about to engage her in. She sat in her seat and stared into her lap, pensive and completely silent. Bram also said nothing.

Picking up on the twosome's reluctance to talk, Mack focused on Vladimir and proceeded to speak, "Well, buddy, it's like this: whether he knew it or not, your brother signed up for a tailored, multi-sequence transgenic hunt. It's also known in some circles as an Evo-Hunt. That's short for Evolving Hunt. What that means is that real-time metrics are applied to the overall hunt from start to finish. Factors including stalk time, shots fired, hit/miss ratios, reaction time, and time to expiration are all evaluated."

It was immediately obvious to Mack that Vladimir had never heard any of this before. The intimidating Russian had all of the trappings of a big-city gangster or crime lord. His alligator boots and silk shirt probably cost more than Mack's entire wardrobe. He wore a Rolex and his shirt sleeves held flashy gold cufflinks. He was well-heeled, but far from well-informed. *Yeah, this is a city slicker through and through*, Mack mused to himself as he continued to explain.

"Evo-hunts used to be staged over months or even years. The clients signed contracts for multiple hunts, each held at set times. The reason being is that it took time to design and produce suitable transgenic species once all the relevant data had been compiled. With the Mega-Preserve, Dr. Fox has somehow eliminated the waiting time. They've created a system that can gather all the data points and then assemble a more challenging game animal. Bigger, faster, stronger, more aggressive, and...more intelligent. Whatever that particular client's needs are, this Gamekeeper can oblige," explained Mack to his now captive audience. "I'm guessing you've decreased the wait time down to a few weeks," finished Mack.

Vladimir looked stunned, almost squeamish. "What do you mean, 'assemble animal'? You mean you make creature in fancy cauldron?"

Seeing that the formerly secret nature of the Mega-Preserve had been disclosed, Dr. Fox no longer felt obliged to remain cautious in her exposition. After all, this was her baby, and she felt an overwhelming need to explain and possibly exonerate herself of wrong-doing. "Mr. O'Boyle has some things correct, Mr. Radovich," she explained. "Other points are pure speculation on his part." The scientist stared at Mack with an air of condescension. Mack O'Boyle may have been a world famous hunter specializing in transgenic species, but she was the transgenic geneticist, the architect of this entire place and everything inside it.

"As to your question," continued Dr. Fox, "the desired game species are produced from undifferentiated cloned specimens held in a proprietary stasis bath. Mr. O'Boyle is correct regarding our facility's data collection system and computerized analysis. What he has grossly underestimated is our turnaround time for specific transgenics. It is not weeks, Mr. O'Boyle; it is only a matter of hours and, sometimes, minutes."

A stunned silence forced its way into the room. Mack stared in shocked wonder at the petite woman as she finished that last statement. *Hours or even minutes? How was that possible? How did they stabilize all of that raw, biological material? What were they using to achieve the needed growth acceleration?* He had been around transgenic species long enough to know that what this woman just boasted about was beyond any technology he had ever encountered. He was certainly impressed by what Fox said, but experience and recent events told him that she and her colleagues had overreached in incalculable ways and the mess confronting them now had been the result.

"You seem pretty proud of yourself, little lady," shot back Mack after he had a moment to gather himself. "Too bad the wheels came off your little science experiment and it is now trying its level best to kill anybody who sets foot in it." Mack motioned over his shoulder with his thumb as he spoke.

"Patchwork freaks made with black magic," muttered Vladimir. "You are a witch, Mrs. Fox, an unholy sorceress."

Fox glared at the looming Russian. "That's Dr. Fox. I have a PhD in genetics and sev..."

"Your CV is not important right now and name calling ain't gonna get us any closer to finding out what happened to the people in the Preserve. We need a rescue plan and we need to execute it ASAP," interrupted Mack. He was still not sold on the idea that transgenics could be mass produced in such a short time. Experience and his gut instinct told him that there must be more to the story. After all, this entire project had been organized and funded by Bram de Jaeger and he was as crooked as the day was long. Anyway, none of these revelations had changed the fact that Michael was missing and he needed help.

Dr. Fox looked incredulous and her heretofore composure and blunt affect suddenly began to crumble. "You can't be serious, O'Boyle," she said angrily. "You want to go inside the Mega-Preserve and launch your own little recovery operation? That's crazy!"

Mack bit his tongue and said nothing back to the suddenly impassioned woman. The formerly mousey scientist had found her big girl voice, and Mack wasn't a huge fan of her shrew-like demeanor. Turning to De Jaeger, he motioned for him to step forward. "I want personnel files on each member of the hunting party, along with a list of their provisions, weapons, and gear. I want their last known coordinates and a detailed physical map of the entire facility."

"Hmmm," noted Vladimir, "I like this man's style. He is not a sniveling dog or evil, crazy witch. You will accompany me on my search for my brother."

"Whoa, now buddy," said Mack looking up with a sense of disbelief in his voice. "How much hunting experience do you have? Have you ever spent an extended amount of time in the wild? Do you or your men know any bushcraft?"

Vladimir's face became red and he stepped up to within inches of Mack's face. "Nyet," snorted the Russian. "I am...how you say...Russian gangster. We do not do crafts in bush. It is waste of time."

The angry man and his men renewed their collective dead-eyed stares at Mack with a reinvigorated menace. Several of his entourage had aggressively begun to flank the old hunter with the obvious intention of intimidating him.

"Listen, Ivan," retorted Mack defiantly in spite of the encroaching circle of ill will. "I don't give two cents who you are or what you're all about in the world. You're about to come face-to-face with the sort of things you've only glimpsed in your worst nightmares. You'll be takin' your life in your own hands."

Mack's bold words seemed to infuriate the Russian. Spit had gathered at the corner of his lips and his nostrils flared out like an angry bull preparing to charge. "You make mistake, little man," growled the re-faced gangster. "My name is Vladimir Mikhail Radovich, not Ivan. You will lead me and my men to find my brother. I fear nothing, especially not stupid animals or old washed-up hunters."

Mack knew he was outnumbered and outgunned. He had to remember why he was here and that the ultimate goal was to find his son. The problem was that this Russian was single-minded and beyond overbearing. He was obviously clueless about what he was about to get himself into, yet he stubbornly maintained an air of righteousness which could only lead to major problems inside the hunting environment.

"Fine," Mack relented. "We can do it your way. Just remember what I said and don't be surprised if things go sideways real quick once we get..."

Mack never had a chance to finish his words of caution. A series of resounding thuds suddenly began to erupt all around the control center. As Mack surveyed the room, he could feel the walls shake and he shook his head sadly. "I thought we might have more time. Looks like we don't..."

"Time?" asked Fox. "What do you mean?"

"We've got incoming, Dr. Fox," said Mack with an unnerving amount of calm. "Grab whatever you can and get ready to head out."

Uncomfortably, the loud thudding sounds continued to reverberate all around them. Radovich's men exploded into a frenetic scramble in an effort to encircle their boss. Yelling at each other in Russian, their stoic, tough guy exteriors had completely dissolved. The hardened enforcers were now lamentably replaced with a group of scared children.

"Nobody is going anywhere," yelled Vladimir. "I..."

Spider-web cracks suddenly began to form on the surface of the wide observation window leading into the Mega-Preserve. A series of several more concentrated thuds were followed by the lightning quick emergence of a dynamite set of gleaming white jaws. Within a matter of seconds, the broken glass gave way entirely and shattered inward, into the darkly lit room in spectacular fashion. In an instant, the whole window's perimeter was surrounded by a multitude of vicious, clamoring bat-like creatures. Each winged horror was the size of a huge German shepherd dog. The snarling monsters each possessed a set of long, curved claws on their front and hind legs, a matching set of long chiropteran-like membranous wings, and their backs were covered in feather-like plumage. Foamy saliva dripped from their snapping muzzles as the outraged throngs of winged beasts began to pour into the control room.

"Flying dogs!" exclaimed Radovich. "I have never seen flying dogs such as these!"

Chapter 6: Flying Dogs, You Say?

"Help me!" yelled De Jaeger
from across the room.

Startled foreign screams erupted from Radovich's men as the entire group began to backpedal away from the snarling horde of airborne terror. As they did, Radovich stalked forward defiantly and began cursing the men in Russian. He was frantically pointing and gesticulating with his hands towards the bizarre threat as the beastly collective scrambled forward through the formerly intact observation window. As he did, his men dutifully produced their weapons and the room erupted in a blaze of noisy gunfire.

Without warning, Mack sprinted towards Dr. Fox and tackled her to the floor. "Keep down!" he yelled as he pushed the young woman beneath a large desk. He then hastily placed a number of overturned chairs in front of her and quickly inspected his makeshift barricade. Once he was convinced that she was secure, Mack carefully raised his head again to survey the exploding chaos. In spite of his years of hunting, not even Mack was prepared for the scene of carnage which greeted him. The giant canine-bat creatures had quickly surged into the control room. Several of them had been killed and/or severely wounded by Radovich's men, but their numbers appeared inexhaustible. The winged abominations continued to stream into the increasingly tight confines of the control room with a psychotic, seemingly unrelenting, reckless abandon.

"Help me!" yelled De Jaeger from across the room. Two of the creatures had taken a hold of his legs and then proceeded to make their way towards the shattered observation window.

"Hang on, Bram," yelled Mack.

Glancing down at his feet, he quickly noticed a prostrate, lifeless body peppered with bite wounds. It was one of Radovich's men. Next to him was a wounded, but defiantly snarling dogbat creature. The dead man was still clutching his blood splattered AK-47 and the barrel was warm. Without a moment's hesitation, Mack bent down and grabbed the assault rifle. As he did, the creature at his feet lunged violently at him and Mack reflexively kicked the animal as hard as he could in the face. The nightmare beast let out a little whimper and then ceased moving altogether.

By now, De Jaeger had been dragged halfway out of the observation window by the duo of dogbats. His legs were flailing wildly and bloody tears were streaming down his terrified face. He moaned and struggled as another of the malevolent creatures quickly joined the others in the collective effort to carry off the battered CEO. The poor man's continued resistance was met with angry bites to the chest and shoulders.

What have you done, Bram? Mack contemplated as he struggled towards the imperiled man. His initial impulse had been to open fire on De Jaeger's aggressors, but the dark horde continued to writhe and gyrate wildly as they unceasingly pulled their captive through the fractured glass opening and into the open air of the Mega-Preserve.

Mack had made it to within five feet of Bram de Jaeger when a contingent of dogbats suddenly swooped down on his position. They now stood between Mack and De Jaeger, forming an impenetrable wall of flapping wings, writhing muscle, and snarling teeth.

Suddenly, as if ordered by some inaudible command, the feral animals rushed forward in a concerted motion. Mack quickly opened fire with his newly procured assault rifle. This was not his accustomed weapons platform, but to Mack, a gun was a gun. Big or small, it didn't matter. He had lived all over the world and shot all types of weapons. Kalashnikov's were all the same: very few bells and whistles; a mass-produced weapon with a really level learning curve; just point, shoot, and rock 'n' roll.

And that's just what Mack did. His ears began to ring prodigiously as he poured round after round into the oversized flying vermin. Head shots were hard given how dynamic and quick the animals were, but Mack soon found he could find the thorax on most of his targets without too much trouble. After only a few seconds, the hunter found himself surrounded by a pile of bloody, winged carcasses with multiple center mass holes. He had incurred a few scratches and minor bruises, but really he was no worse for the wear.

Mack scanned the littered corpses and it suddenly occurred to him that he could no longer hear Bram's screams. Looking up, a sick feeling overtook him. The pit in his stomach grew more and more noticeable as he desperately searched the immediate vicinity for any trace of De Jaeger. No, he saw nothing. He was nowhere to be found. *Had they really flown away with him? Why would they do that?*

Further scanning the room, Mack was once again shocked by the level of carnage. Human bodies were intermixed with those of the dead animal assailants. A bloodied Radovich was sitting in an office chair, tending to a terrible bite wound on his right leg.

"Vladimir? Are you ok?" questioned Mack as he surveyed the scene for other possible survivors.

"Nyet, Mr. Hunter, I am not alright," retorted the enraged man. "Flying dogs killed my men and bit me on the leg. I now have hole in my designer French pants. They are, how you say, custom."

Radovich was right. His men had all been wiped out. The silence in the room was still punctuated by the dying wails of the winged animals, but aside from Mack and the Russian, not a single other human being appeared to still be alive. In a few short minutes, the control room had been transformed into a literal abattoir. Mack shook his head in disgust at the loss of life.

"H-help me," exclaimed a tiny female voice from beneath a disheveled desk in the anterior part of the control room.

Fox! Mack anxiously thought as he whirled around and ran to inspect the impromptu hiding space he had fashioned for the geneticist. Bending down, Mack quickly set to work removing the dead dogbat creatures from the floor in front of the desk. The chairs, which had been meant to serve as a makeshift barricade, were now a tangled prison of torn fabric, bent metal, and bloodied transgenic animal fur. As Mack did his best to evacuate the crimson-splattered monster corpses from the area, he caught a glimpse of Dr. Fox's face. Her eyes appeared to be frozen open in an unblinking stare and her cheeks looked as if they were drained of all vitality. Her dress and lab coat were smeared with blood and she had bits of bone and fur in her hair as well as on her forehead.

"Are you ok?" exclaimed Mack with sincere concern. "Are you hurt?"

Fox said nothing. She continued to gaze off at an unknown point in the distance, totally shell-shocked and unable to utter a word.

"Th-they're attacking us," she managed to mutter in a faraway voice. "Gamekeeper is trying to k-k-kill us."

Mack almost felt sorry for the woman. She was emotionally devastated and the level of disappointment in her voice was obvious. Her greatest professional accomplishment had somehow decided to turn on its creator and kill everyone in the facility. It had to be a bitter pill to swallow. "Dr. Fox," said Mack, "we have to go. If we stay here, we're dead."

Josephine Fox continued to stare off into space for a brief time, and then, in a sudden moment of clarity, she turned to the old hunter and nodded her head. Mack took her by the hand and quickly led her towards the doorway.

"Where are you going, O'Boyle?" asked Radovich as Mack was about the open the heavy metal door leading to the stairwell.

"We need to resupply and regroup," said Mack. "I need to get Fox somewhere safe and you need medical. Those bat-things will be back any minute. Can you walk?"

Radovich scrutinized his bloody clothes and the series of bite wounds along his arm and leg. "Da," muttered the injured Russian, reverting to his native tongue momentarily. "I can walk..."

However, as Mack proceeded to pull open the big door, he was immediately greeted by a group of low howls and primal screams. There, clamoring on top of each other

73

throughout the stairwell was another army of dogbat creatures, each coiled and ready to spring into action.

As Mack's eyes locked onto those of the creature closest to him, he attempted to slam the door shut, but he was not quick enough. Two of the winged monsters managed to insert their heads between the heavy door and the door jam. Mack strenuously pushed back against the horde of terror with all his power, but he was beyond tired and could feel the writhing bodies begin to successfully make their way through the narrow opening inch by inch. Their crazed blood-shot eyes, snapping teeth, and arched necks spasmed and strained unrelentingly until they were not even a foot away from Mack's right thigh.

Josephine Fox could see what was happening and, gathering all her strength, rallied to Mack's aid. As she pressed up against the door, she could feel the unceasing push of the unnaturally forceful creatures on the other side.

"They're in the stairwell," yelled Mack. "We have no way out. Dr. Fox, if we don't get this door shut, we're all dead. There must be at least fifty of those things on the other side. Can you reach my gun?"

"Y-yes," she stammered.

Fox slowly reached for the AK slung over Mack's shoulder, carefully began to pull it towards herself, and prepared to discharge it when a barely audible slushing sound suddenly emanated from the narrow opening to the stairwell. This was followed by another and another.

Looking around, Mack noticed that the big Russian had silently crept towards the door opening and somehow decapitated the monstrous intruders with his menacing knife. The snarling ensemble of intrusive snapping teeth and guttural howls was partially silenced as the trio of lifeless heads fell onto the control room floor. Crimson fluids began to seep around the threshold as the hellacious canine-like intruders' now headless bodies fell backwards into the stairwell opening.

Mack simultaneously felt a substantial release of pressure from the other side of the door. With a revitalized sense of vigor, Mack pushed into the cumbersome metal framed opening with all of his might and, seconds later, felt a resounding thud and a powerful click.

The door, by some miracle, was now thankfully closed. Mack slid down to the floor like a crumpled rag-doll and sat motionless for a few brief moments. Off to his right, Mack noticed that the floor had become exceptionally bloody, and in the center of the ever-expanding sticky red pool stretched out Radovich's prostrate form. In his still tightly clenched right hand was the menacing knife he had wielded so mightily just a short time ago. It was caked with blood and fur, and the distal tip of the dangerous looking weapon was now broken off. All around Radovich lay the disarticulated body parts of the dogbat creatures. Teeth, bisected jaws, and ears lay strewn about in a macabre, random pattern.

"Flying dogs have hard heads, but I wield Russian steel, Mr. Hunter," explained Vladimir Radovich weakly as he cast his eyes towards Mack. "You shut the door?"

"Yeah," replied Mack. "Nice work with the pig sticker," he said as he motioned to the scene of carnage surrounding the Russian and the entryway to the stairwell.

"My grandfather was butcher in St. Petersburg. I help him sometimes in my youth. We cut up cows, pigs, sheep, but no flying dogs," said Vladimir with a wry smile.

Mack's mind's eye quickly conjured up an image of a young Vladimir Radovich chopping away with an oversized meat cleaver in his family's butcher shop. A series of distasteful images then began to flood his head as he remembered what he had heard about the Radovich's infamous crime organization. The Russians were well-known for their use of knives and cutting implements when it came to dealing with their rivals and anyone else who did not toe the line. Mack found it darkly ironic that such a decidedly anti-social skill set had just saved their lives.

"Well," proclaimed Mack as he quickly scanned the room for further threats, "looks like we aren't going out the way we came."

"What do you suggest then?" asked Dr. Fox as she did her best to adjust her torn and bloody ensemble. "You don't seriously think we can go in there," she finished as she pointed into the forbidding Mega-Preserve.

"I don't see any other option," countered Mack. "We can't stay here. We're sitting ducks and your turncoat computer program obviously knows it. The elevator is down, and we already tried to go out the stairwell and that's crawling with hostiles. Our best bet is to supply up here as best we can and hump it into the Preserve. We stay out of sight and do our best to avoid trouble. While we're in there, we look for survivors and try to help anybody we can who is still alive."

Dr. Fox was shaking her head. This entire situation had long ago spun out of control and she simply wanted to get as far away from this place as possible. She recognized the evolving dangers inside the Mega-Preserve better than anyone and the idea of going into the belly of the beast was simply unthinkable.

"No!" she replied. "We'll never make it more than a few yards. Everybody who has gone in there has died. I know what is waiting for us inside. I designed this entire biosphere, from every blade of grass to the largest transgenic pachyderm. I won't do it!"

Mack took a moment to wipe the sweat from his eyes. He was tired, dog tired, and fighting with this weird scientist was the last thing he wanted to do right now.

"Yeah, sweetheart," said Mack derisively, "you really have outdone yourself. Grade A job. The dogbats were a very nice touch."

"I had nothing to do with those things," retorted Dr. Fox. "They are not my designs. I would..."

"Never design something like this?" yelled Mack as he bent down and quickly heaved up one of the deceased bat creatures by the nape of the neck. "Hmmm," he said as he inspected the dead animal. "I'm seeing a chiropteric base, probably giant fruit bat." Mack pulled the jaws apart and inspected the animal's mouth. "This dentition is lupine and the eyes and ears are decidedly feline. Not only that, but the claws are retractable." Mack then grabbed a broken femur and peered into the open fracture midway along the shaft. "Oh, and the bones are hypertrabeculated. It looks like somebody threw in some raptor genes for good measure."

"If you did not, then who did this?" asked Radovich as he continued to reinforce the metal door with office debris and overturned furniture. A continuous knocking sound could be heard coming from the stairwell as the remaining frenzied creatures pressed unrelentingly forward.

Mack continued to inspect the dead animal. Even though he lacked any formal forensic training and held no advanced degrees, the old hunter had seen more than his fair share of dead transgenics. That fact, coupled with a lifelong interest in autodidacticism made him truly question the nature of this creature and its overall role in the preceding events.

"No, she's tellin' the truth, Vladimir," declared Mack suddenly as he allowed the dead beast to slump to the floor. "No company concerned with profits would ever go to the trouble of making an animal like this for a recreational hunt. I'm convinced these babies are the work of a freelancer. This is a mission-specific animal, a transgenic soldier designed to operate aerially, infiltrate an elevated space, and be strong, flexible, and aggressive."

"Soldier?" asked Vladimir not sure he had heard correctly.

"Yep," said Mack. "I think Dr. Fox is responsible for this nonsense insofar as she helped create the Mega-Preserve and refined the production capabilities."

Josephine Fox shot a caustic, choleric visage at both Radovich and Mack. Her arms were folded and she looked upset.

"That being said," continued Mack, "her creation is now acting completely independently and showing a level of decision making and design that scares the heck out of me. Bottom line is that we have no choice but to head into the belly of the beast, literally, and find whoever is alive and shut this whole thing down."

"And how do you propose to do that?" sneered Dr. Fox. "You admitted yourself that you don't even know who or what has taken control of Gamekeeper. You'd be operating blindly."

Mack was silent for a moment. She was right. He didn't know who or what had taken control of this place. He was a hunter with a wide range of skills, but he was not an academic, a trained scientist, or an experienced computer programmer. His world and the problems inside it were usually best answered with simple, straightforward responses.

"The birthing chamber and the generators," answered Mack. "You disrupt either one of them and we significantly slow or altogether incapacitate this place's ability to hurt us."

"Ah, I see what you mean," exclaimed Radovich. "Turn off the lights or turn off the...how you say...spicket? Yes?"

"Yeah, that's what I'm thinkin'," replied Mack.

Fox was still vigorously shaking her head. While the men spoke, she grabbed several hardcopy maps and spread them out on the crimson-splattered console. "We are here, in Sector 1," reported Fox as she struck the top right-hand portion of the map with a rigid, pointed index finger. "The Birthing House is located here, in Sector 19," she said as her hand flew across the map to the lower left-hand corner of the unfolded piece of paper. "That is over thirty miles full of active water and rocky terrain, and who knows what kind of transgenics. Oh, and you wanted to take out the emergency power supply? Well, guess what?" she said in an insincere, snide fashion. "It's located in the subbasement of this very building. There is a separate

79

major substation here," she said motioning to the map, "But it is at elevation and located about 3 miles from the Birthing House, all the way over here." Once again, Fox's hand slid along the map to the extreme lower left-hand corner of the map. "No matter how you slice it, we have to cross the Mega-Preserve," she continued. "It would take an army to do that. We..."

A loud groaning sound had been steadily building as Fox was explaining her concerns. Radovich's hastily produced barricade of chairs and computer debris began to heave and sway as the pitched animal screams grew louder and louder.

"Listen, princess," said Mack, "big bats are gettin' in. Time to fish or cut bait. We go in there," Mack said, pointing over his shoulder at the vast wilderness behind him, "and we might die. If we stay here and go another round with those things, we will most assuredly be killed."

"I am with you, O'Boyle," said Radovich as he stooped down and collected several partially loaded magazines from discarded weapons. "The flying dogs are coming, Dr. Lady. Stay here if you like to die. I'm going to find my brother, Vasilli."

Fox's face writhed with an expression of disbelief and fear. The situation had spun completely out of control. De Jaeger was gone and most likely dead. Everything now seemed to be far beyond their ability to manage. Her greatest professional triumph had rapidly descended into a chaotic nightmare. She was terrified of dying a violent death inside the control room, but the unknown horrors lurking inside the Preserve conveyed the impression of being just as forbidding.

Mack could sense that the female scientist's capitulation was only deepening. Ideally, he would just take off and go find his son on his own. The crazy Russian gangster was no doubt a liability, but Dr. Fox was proving herself to be a real pain in the neck. "I'm about done here, Doc," warned Mack. "Time's a-wastin' and I have a plan. Either you get with the program or you stay here and get eaten."

Fox looked irritated, but said nothing. Radovich just smiled as he watched the old hunter dress down the scientist. "You and De Jaeger tried Control/Alt/Delete and it ain't workin' so we need a different approach."

"So," Dr. Fox retorted, "you want to go and die on some foolish quest with a half-baked plan to..."

"Stop," interjected Mack. "Just stop talking and listen." Mack's eyes narrowed to little slits and his cheeks were red. "You're thinking like a scientist, a computer geek," said Mack. "You're not thinking like a hunter. Even the most dangerous animals in the world have behavior patterns and specific weaknesses that can be exploited. You helped build this place, Dr. Fox. You could be a real asset if you decided to get off X and make a decision."

With that, Mack turned to Radovich and motioned to De Jaeger's now empty office. "Maps show a side stairwell leading from that office to the Preserve entrance. We take that way down and pray to God that we don't find any unfortunate surprises. Once we get inside, we stay tight to the dense foliage to avoid the bigger organisms."

Radovich nodded and both men stared back at Fox. She was holding the AK-47 Mack had acquired earlier, keeping herself busy inspecting the weapon. "So," mused

Radovich, "you come with us? Ha! Have you used Comrade Kalashnikov's most perfect weapon before?"

"My father was a Special Forces Weapons Sergeant," Fox stated coyly. "He taught me how to shoot." Fox said nothing more as she slung the rifle over her shoulder, seemingly resigned to this course of action.

A look of pleasant surprise snuck up onto Mack's face. "I'll be dipped," he said as he inspected the petite woman and the automatic rifle. "You're a woman of many talents."

As the group of three turned to exit the abandoned office and make their way down the narrow stairs, Mack noticed a massive gun suspended from the wall behind De Jaeger's desk. ".600 Nitro...," he muttered as he stopped to look at the weapon.

"What is that?" asked Vladimir.

".600 Nitro Express," replied Mack. "It's one of the big boys. Lots of fellas don't like it or the .577 because of the kick. They've been known to dislocate the lenses in people's eyes. I've found it to be helpful on lots of medium-sized transgenics. This is a good find."

Mack reached over and took the sizable weapon down from its perch on the wall. After that, he reached down and pulled open a broad top drawer from a wide mahogany desk. "Bram always was predictable," mused Mack as he pulled out a big box of .600 ammunition. The jumbo bullets made a blunted jingling sound as he set the container on top of the messy desk and began to load the massive gun. With a resounding click, he closed the breech to the double rifle and then placed the cigar-shaped bullets into his bloodstained satchel.

The trio then warily descended the tight accessory stairway with muted caution. During their descent, they could hear the occasional sound of scratching claws and guttural echoes reverberate throughout the concrete enclosure.

"When we get to the service door," whispered Mack, "I'll take a look. If the coast is clear, we head in. Keep your eyes peeled." Both Radovich and Fox nodded solemnly.

When the group emerged from behind the heavy stairway door, they were greeted by a lush rainforest scene brimming with grandiose palmated plants, dense grasses, tall hardwood trees, and the incessant buzzing of insects. As the party scanned the area before them, they were each assailed by a mixture of foreign smells and hot, humid air.

"Looks like we are good to go," breathed Mack.

Cautiously, the hunter and his two companions made their way through the thick foliage, and, as they did, Mack could not help but be impressed. The trees, insects, and undergrowth seemed familiar, yet somehow different. This place reminded him of all the places he had ever hunted during his long career, yet it still held an otherworldly appeal that he could not fully understand. Only moments ago, the group had barely survived a deadly animal attack. People were killed, kidnapped, and injured. His son was lost, now possibly dead, in a place that had quickly become the most dangerous locale on earth. In spite of that, Mack felt a sense of wonder and curiosity as he drank in his unique surroundings. For someone who had been all over the world and in every natural setting imaginable, this place was very special and unlike any he had ever dreamt of.

The trio continued walking on in silence for several more minutes. Dr. Fox grew increasingly nervous as they continued. The further the group walked, the more she began to question her decision to brave the dangers of the Preserve. She was visibly anxious and said nothing as her eyes roved warily back and forth across the jungle expanse. She clutched the AK-47 tightly to her chest, her fingernails nearly digging into the wooden stock.

Radovich also confirmed that he was completely out of his element. Bulbous beads of sweat streamed down his face and he continually made a swiping motion across his forehead with the back of his torn shirt sleeve. The Russian's demeanor reminded Mack of all the other wise guys and criminals he had met in his life. Each one, without exception, always tried to use intimidation and fear to get what they wanted. They would threaten and use violence to control their environments and the people within them, until they ended up outside their comfort zone. When the situation called for more than just simple thuggery, these hard men would devolve into scared little kids. No matter what their particular nationality, it was always the same.

Mack's minor bemusement was suddenly interrupted when he noticed a broken radio on the ground. From the looks of it, something very fierce had savagely bitten the device in two. It was smeared with saliva and blood. Gazing up, Mack quickly noticed a trail of broken tactical equipment and discarded weapons. Drops of blood were splattered about and torn military-style uniforms were intermixed among the strewn debris.

"Oh no! This is what I was afraid of... Arvid...," muttered Mack as he scanned the debris.

"What is it?" asked Fox as she peered over Mack's shoulder.

A look of terror mixed with disgust quickly came into view on the scientist's face. Her cheeks lost all color and she looked as though she might vomit.

"It's Russell's team," replied Mack. "It looks like they didn't get very far."

Radovich quickly moved up to view the macabre scene. Swiping a thick, hairy arm across his perpetually perspiring forehead, he stood in stunned silence for several seconds. "Bozhe moi, what could have done this?" he managed to say after his initial shock.

"Transgenics, Mr. Radovich," replied Mack in a matter-of-fact way, "mean 'ol transgenics."

Chapter 7: Behemoths Afoot

"Bram always did like the idea of making a King Kong for his own personal pet."

"This was your friend?" Radovich inquired. "He was strong soldier, yes?"

"Yeah, he was about as well-trained as you can get," replied Mack sadly. "Being a colonel in the South African Special Forces, he was an experienced hunter himself. His team was made up of special operations types as well. "

"And now they're all dead. I told you!" screeched Dr. Fox as her nerves gave way and she shot a venomous look towards Mack. "What hope do we have of surviving in here if Arvid Russel and his trained killers couldn't? You've doomed us all. We will die here; it's just a matter of time! You're a 60-year-old over-the-hill hunter and you think you can shut this place down? You're crazy! It was so stupid to come here!"

Mack looked furious. He had hoped Fox would be an asset given her scientific background and the significant role she had played in creating the Preserve. She showed some common sense and a bit of grit a few minutes ago, but her outburst indicated that she was going to have trouble keeping it together.

"You listen to me, lady," growled Mack with a dark tone. "Number 1: Keep your voice down or the things that got Russell's group will be all over us. Number 2: You're just like every other egghead scientist I've met over my career. You think you know everything, but really you only know everything about nothing. You can't hide behind your PhD and compute or hypothesize your way out of this. You and your boss created one huge mess. It's gonna take some outside the box thinking to solve this. Russell's team thought they could come loaded for bear and shoot their way out of here. That didn't happen and it ain't happening now."

"What do you mean by that?" asked Radovich.

"Look around, Vladimir," said Mack. "What do you see?"

Radovich surveyed the violent scene and shrugged his shoulders. "I see death and destruction," said the Russian.

"Yeah, you're not wrong about that, but there's more," said Mack as he motioned towards the ground. "Look at the spoor all around this site," muttered Mack.

"Spoor?" questioned Vladimir. "What is this 'spoor' you speak of?"

"Tracks, Vlad, animal tracks," replied Mack as he pointed to the ground.

Bending down, Mack placed his hand next to a liberal indentation in the soil. It measured about 30 centimeters across and 3 centimeters deep. "This is a wide track," continued Mack. "It's a cloved hoof and looks a lot like a cape buffalo's, but the thing is three times bigger than any dugga boy spoor I've ever seen."

"I know what you are getting at, Mr. O'Boyle," stammered Dr. Fox. "I can tell you that this facility does not have the potential to produce what you're talking about. Again, it is far beyond our safety protocols."

"Yeah," Mack chortled. "Just like the ferocious flying dogbats back in the control room."

"Like I said," fired back Fox, "those designs are not mine. They're not part of any hunting algorithm in the Preserve. You know as well as I do how dangerous these creatures can be. I would never design behemoths for a recreational hunting facility. Gamekeeper has safeguards to prevent such things."

"Ba-he-moth?" queried Radovich. "You people use strange words."

"Behemoths, Vlad," explained Mack, "from the Bible, Book of Job. The transgenic industry agreed that they should never be produced. They have always been a theoretical danger because the sheer amount of biological material needed was a major stumbling block to producing them."

"You are talking about big hunting animals?" asked the Russian.

"Big?" Mack replied. "Yeah, you could say that. The African elephant is the largest land animal on earth. We're talking about animals orders of magnitude larger and three times tougher. If this place is producing behemoths, it means things just got a whole lot more dangerous."

"Bram always did like the idea of making a King Kong for his own personal pet," continued Mack. "De Jaeger Enterprises was planning to build an entire weapons line focused on hunting them. I know because I was consulted on it five years ago. The R and D boys made a mini-behemoth combining elements of a hippo, bison, and crocodile. The thing stood about twelve feet high at the shoulders and weighed 30 tons. They told me it was just a first attempt and that they had plans to make these things enormous."

"When the company initiated the final testing phase, absolute chaos broke loose. It killed its handlers, escaped, and went rogue outside of Kruger Park. I went in, along with a few other professional hunters and tracked the beast down. It wiped out two of the five teams sent in after it and killed a number of civilians as well. We finally engaged the thing just outside the park and barely killed it. It shrugged off the .50 cal rounds like they were nothing. We ended up using military ordinance to disable it and finally set the thing on fire. De Jaeger had to pay out some serious money to keep it all hush-hush."

"So my brother was sent into this place to hunt unstoppable killing machines? Is that what you are telling me? Crazy witch doctor!" growled Radovich as he cast an accusing eye towards Dr. Fox.

"Relax, Vlad" said Mack as he tried to step between the Russian and the scared geneticist. "Fox says she didn't make them and we have to give her the benefit of the doubt. We know more now than we did before. The first hunting lodge should be less than 5 miles north of here. We need shelter or we are dead meat. There should be food there as well. I know I'm gettin' hungry. Our best tactic is to stay hidden and not to directly engage..."

While Mack was talking, Vladimir appeared completely indifferent to his instructions. He had brazenly turned his back on the old hunter and made his way towards an area of heavy jungle overgrowth. Scanning the wild space before him, he marched forward and his massive frame was quickly obscured by the vegetation.

Watching the Russian's disrespectful display, Mack angrily growled, "Hey, are you listening to me?" but his voice was suddenly drowned out by a series of gun shots.

Then, Vladimir victoriously emerged holding a showy purple bird with black highlights to its wings and a thick red crest on its head. "Ha!" yelled out Radovich as he held up the bullet-riddled fowl. "Are you not great hunter,

O'Boyle? Why do you not hunt and eat creatures in the make-believe jungle? I show you how it is done. What do you think of my bushcraft now, Mr. American Hunter?"

Mack and Dr. Fox could only look on in dismay as the big man began to pull the turkey-sized creature apart. Their position had been given away to anyone who cared to notice. They were sitting ducks.

As Radovich continued to tug and wrestle with the foreign looking bird carcass, Mack took in his surroundings carefully. The transgenic that had killed Arvid Russell's team could still be in the vicinity. If it was a behemoth that got to Arvid and his men, they probably did not realize it was on them until it was far too late. That had been the big takeaway outside Kruger: despite their unbelievable size, behemoths could be fast and exceedingly quiet.

Radovich had managed to pull a leg and a wing off the dead bird. A cloud of feathers enveloped his solid frame and he motioned to Fox with the disarticulated bird femur.

"Here, witch doctor woman," said Radovich in a matter-of-fact way. "You pluck plentiful chicken and make fire. I will go and shoot more food." The Russian gangster turned and began to trudge back into the heavy underbrush with his gun held high. Mack was about to protest when he was interrupted by the sound of unholy growls mixed with high-pitched guttural grunting.

Radovich froze in his tracks. Several dark, monstrous shadows emerged over his silhouette. As they grew taller and taller, he began to feel more and more diminutive. Looking up slowly, Vladimir locked eyes with a sinister appearing set of yellow orbs. They were glittering, bioluminescent, unblinking, and belonging to a face that could only be described as the stuff of nightmares.

The animal snorted and then let out another series of growls. Orange-colored saliva dripped from its gaping, tusk-filled mouth. Its protruding nostrils flared in and out in a streak of spastic movements. Muscles bulged and heaved along its thick neck, and its mountainous, black body swayed back and forth with an agitated urgency that could only mean impending death.

Radovich, for his part, said not a word and did not twitch a muscle. It was as if an unholy terror had seized hold of his mind and he could think and do nothing. He was now trapped in his own body. As the deadly beast continued forward, the gangster continued to stare straight ahead, clutching the dead foul tightly.

The massive transgenic suddenly lowered its head and began to shift its body weight onto its front legs. Deafeningly, the entire scene was punctuated by a loud "Kaboom!" followed by another loud gunshot. The large monster stepped back with a look of utter bewilderment on its face. It quickly reoriented itself towards the source of its pain and began to charge.

Mack had already broken open the breach on the .600 Nitro Express double rifle and was reloading the heavy-duty bullets. He then closed the immense gun with a resounding "click" and hoisted it up to his right shoulder once again. "You two get the heck out of here," yelled Mack as he took aim a second time. "We can't outrun this thing!"

Upon hearing Mack's words, Radovich suddenly regained his presence of mind. He turned and lumbered away from the monster with an awkward, loping gait. "Here!" he screamed as he trudged forward, "Take dead chicken for your own!"

"You can't stay here!" yelled Fox as the Russian accelerated past her. "You had to use explosives on the last behemoths you encountered."

Mack said nothing in reply as the deafening roar of the .600 Nitro Express erupted yet another time. The formidable creature staggered back for only a moment, dazed, but not at all incapacitated. It then stomped forward, twice as determined.

Mack grabbed Fox by the wrist and began to drag the petite woman towards the thicker underbrush. "I need to outflank this thing and make a decent shot on its ear or near an eye. Stay here!"

"You're going to do what?" screamed Josephine Fox, certain that she could not possibly have heard the old hunter correctly.

Not bothering to acknowledge the question, Mack jumped up and made a beeline towards the dangerous animal with the heavy gun pointed straight up in the air. When he was within 50 yards of the creature, he delivered a straight-on gun shot that found its way into the attacking animal's center of mass.

The nightmare beast furiously rose up in anger and let out a tremendous scream. Then, it surged forward towards the source of its pain undeterred, but Mack remained in continuous motion. With no time to lose, he quickly jogged off at a 45-degree angle, all the while keeping an eye on the lumbering creature over his shoulder. When he was approximately 30 yards away, he once again whirled around and proceeded to let loose with the powerful double rifle. "Kaboom...Kaboom!"

The behemoth creature spun around in an impossibly tight semi-circle. As it uttered a series of horrible growls, Fox could tell something had changed. The previously menacing animal's movements were now slower and its level of aggression seemed to have been dulled slightly. The creature's hind quarters began to shudder and tremble as its tail flopped towards the ground.

Suddenly, with no warning other than a great heaving motion in the chest, the animal raised itself up to its full height and then came crashing down to the jungle floor with a resounding thud. It let out one last horrible gasp and then ceased to move all together. A final throbbing fibrillation made its way through the once active creature's frame and then there was nothing. It was dead.

Following a lighting fast reload, Mack slowly approached the dead beast with his rifle raised. Warily, he made his way to the monstrous horned head, gave it a kick and then a slight nudge with the tip of his heavy gun. A crimson pool began to form itself next to the dead animal's gross cranial cavity. A closer inspection revealed a moderate trickle of bright red blood that emerged from both the left eye and the left ear.

Fox made her way out of the makeshift hiding place. She was shaking badly, but could not contain her curiosity. Somehow, the unkillable had been killed.

"You made the shots...," she stammered in thinly veiled disbelief. "You actually killed it."

Mack said nothing for a moment. He was out of breath and still trying to recover from the terrifying ordeal. "Well,

Dr. Fox," replied Mack. "I didn't have much choice. This big boy is armor-plated." To demonstrate, Mack stuck his fingers into the holes made by the .600 Nitro. He had struck the creature twice in the thorax, but was only able to bury his finger in just past the nail bed.

"No penetration, Doc," he discerned as he inspected the wound and the truncated channel. "The last one of these was smaller, but just as tough. Only way to penetrate the brain case was through the middle ear or into the orbit. St. Hubertus had my back."

Mack turned his attention to the creature's massive cranium. As he reached his hand along the left ear, he was greeted by a slow trickle of bright red blood. The .600 bullet had found its mark directly into the external auditory canal. It had obliterated the middle and inner ear cavities and Mack could only assume that the projectile had entered the temporal lobe of the terrorizing transgenic's brain. Where it may have tumbled from there was anybody's guess. Obviously, it had been enough to remove the threat and save their lives.

Satisfied and relieved to still be alive, Mack reached into his shirt and kissed the worn medal hanging from his neck. He then dutifully replaced the object beneath his sweat-soaked clothes.

"St. Hubertus?" wondered Dr. Fox as Mack ushered the two of them into the deeper jungle.

"Patron saint of hunters," said Mack in reply. "I ask him for help sometimes."

Dr. Fox let out a poorly concealed chuckle. Religion was for superstitious, stupid people. No real scientist believed in saints and God and organized religion. It was all a waste of time as far as she was concerned.

"I'm not surprised by your response, Doctor," said Mack as he marched forward. "You scientists tend to be a godless bunch. It's probably the underlying reason we're in this situation right now. None of you believes in natural law or in anything to do with God's Plan. You all know best, spending your lives chasin' money and the approval of your peers, never thinkin' about what the Lord wants you to be doing instead."

It was immediately obvious that Dr. Fox was not pleased by the older man's assessment. Mack had just saved her life, but she did not see in any way how God or some obscure saint had had anything to do with it. Yes, the transgenic was a monster, but it was a manmade monster and had been stopped by a man using manmade weapons. The need to insert some sort of divine intervention into the scenario seemed unnecessary at best and absolutely anti-intellectual at worst. "Hmmm," mumbled Fox as she looked slyly at Mack, "I do not pretend to understand, but to each his own."

Mack said nothing in return. She seemed like a lost cause and their collective survival was still foremost on his mind. After all, Mack was far from a devout Christian and God only knew all of the bad things he had done in his life. Evangelizing some twit scientist in the middle of a death trap was obviously a bad idea. He needed to remain focused on the task at hand. Still, Fox's lack of even rudimentary faith was grating, but not altogether unexpected given what he had observed of the woman so far.

Mack and Dr. Fox soon caught up with Radovich. He still looked visibly shaken and said nothing as the duo approached.

"You nearly got us all killed back there," announced Mack with narrowed eyes and a harsh, accusatory tone in his voice. "You're in my world now, buddy, and you better start getting used to it. You don't do a single thing unless I tell you to. Do you understand me?"

Upon hearing these words, Vladimir clenched his fists and gritted his teeth. He was a proud Russian and a man of action, but it was now unmistakable to him just how out of his element he truly was. This foreign environment was nothing like the mean streets of Moscow in which he was the ultimate predator. Here, in this artificial wilderness, he was nothing more than a scared forest creature, reduced to running in terror from the horrible beings who called this foreboding place home. "Da," replied the Russian after a moment of uncomfortable silence. "You are boss in charge...the czar of this crazy jungle. I will do as you say."

"Good," said Mack. He did not gloat or take any pleasure in dressing down Radovich. His first order of business was to maintain order and put an end to any future freelancing. Hopefully, Vlad had gotten the message and would observe the chain of command from here on out. "C'mon," said Mack, "we've got at least a 2 hour hike to the lodge. From there, hopefully we can eat, resupply, and make plans."

"It won't work," emerged a voice from the background. "It's a good plan, but it won't succeed."

The weary trio whirled around to see an Asian man standing behind him. He was wearing tattered clothes and cradled a worn rifle in his arms. At his side was a long, thin knife with a red jewel in the hilt. He had a sparse beard and his jet black hair was pulled back tightly against his skull. "Your son suggested the same thing, Mr. O'Boyle: get to a lodge, resupply, avoid the larger species, and try to disable the Preserve's power."

"Mr. Tanaka, I presume?" asked Mack.

"Yes," said the thin, athletic man as he scampered down a small embankment. "Matsumo Tanaka, at your service," he said, bowing courteously to the group and then peering intently at each of the three individuals before him. His eyes immediately locked onto Mack's and did not look away. He seemed to be studying him, as if he had been waiting in anticipation for this moment for some time.

"Where's my son?" said Mack, not wasting any time getting down to business.

"Your son?" replied Tanaka. "I do not know the answer to your question. The last time I saw Dr. O'Boyle, he was trying to save Mr. Dominguez from an angry leopard creature. I fear they are both dead."

A stunned silence came over Mack. A flushed wave of anxiety mixed with fear suddenly shook his body to the core, but he quickly collected himself.

"But you didn't see him killed?" said Mack. "You didn't see a body?"

"That is correct," replied Tanaka. "Our group was overwhelmed with transgenics relatively early on. We had suffered several attacks when Dominguez was cut off from the rest of us. Your son ran to help him, but I cannot confirm his success or failure."

"Why didn't you help him?" shot back Mack who was barely able to hide his anger at the thought that the group of hunters had abandoned his son.

"Your son instructed us to flee," responded Tanaka with an emotionless tone. "Mr. Dominguez was already wounded and your son's instructions were to get to safety. He planned to rendezvous with us later once he had rescued him."

Mack was hard pressed to tell if the Asian was lying. In his experience, most people demonstrated specific "tells" when they lied or told half-truths. Tanaka's eyes never deviated and his face remained featureless. He was either telling the truth or he was an expert at hiding it.

"Why didn't you evacuate to the lodges or try to get to the generators?" asked Mack with suspicion.

"Ah, yes, you are referencing the generators along the plateau region," nodded Tanaka with a knowing look. "We were pursued and prevented from making our way north," he replied in a calm voice. "Hendrick Gruber and Vasilli Radovich were killed by a pack of...hyena-lizard...animals."

A look of utter dismay came over Vladimir's face. "My brother...killed?" he stammered. "You saw this with your own eyes?"

Tanaka seemed unfazed and almost cold in his treatment of the violent events that had transpired in the Preserve. "Yes, I did. They were both killed along with their PHs," he replied. "This place, this Mega-Preserve, has no permanent safe havens. Nothing is beyond its reach. The jungle produces hellish otherworldly creatures, creatures I would not have believed had I not seen them with my own eyes."

99

"Kinda like huge flying dogs and pachyderms as humongous as semi-trucks?" Mack agreed.

"Yes. That is exactly what I am talking about," said Tanaka. "There is nowhere to run, nowhere to hide. This place will find you. It always finds a solution to the problem of your continued existence."

"Which begs the question," followed-up Mack, "how did you, a total novice, survive when the rest of your group is supposedly dead? Beginner's luck?"

Mack found himself feeling very suspicious. *This Tanaka is one odd duck*, contemplated Mack. *There is no way he is who he says he is.* Mack had combed over any available information regarding the men in his son's hunting party. He was already familiar with most of the clients. The other men in the group were known commodities: criminals, oddballs, and sociopaths. This Japanese man stood out as an anomaly. With no hunting background to speak of, the fact that he was still alive was difficult to comprehend. The idea that there was more to this man than meets the eye was becoming more and more likely the longer their interaction occurred. The bottom line was that something simply did not smell right about this guy.

"You have a valid point, Mr. O'Boyle," said Tanaka with his continued unnerving calmness. "The only places that offer some minimal protection are the rock formations located throughout the Preserve. I avoided direct confrontation with the larger species by hiding in the crevices and small caves. The smaller predators I had to deal with in a more direct manner." Tanaka then motioned to a nearby rock. On it were strewn the motionless bodies of a number of snakelike creatures. Each had been bludgeoned about the head and a small area of blood stain was visible around the sunken-in craniums.

"Looks like you had to learn the ropes quickly," said Mack skeptically.

Again, there was yet no trace of emotion on the Japanese man's face. He turned from the rest of the group and looked directly at Mack. "Yes, I had to adapt to my surroundings and act quickly. I did what I had to do in order to survive and control the situation."

Tanaka continued to stare back at Mack as he spoke. His face never gave way to any signs of stress or overt emotion. Further questions seemed to be futile at this point and Mack was eager to continue on, especially given the revelation regarding Michael's last known whereabouts.

"Well," said Mack, "my son may still be alive. If the rest of you want to hide out here, I don't blame you. I'm going into the interior."

Tanaka continued to stare at Mack with the same cold, penetrating eyes and expressionless visage. He did not smile, nor did he frown. Everything about the man was neutral and utterly mysterious. "You should know," interjected Tanaka as Mack began to gather himself to leave, "your son told me that the only man who could survive in this place was his father. Unfortunately, not even you can stop what is about to happen."

Fox stepped forward. She had been listening to Tanaka speak and also had many questions as to how he had survived in the Preserve when so many others had gone missing or had been killed. The nervous man she had encountered before the hunt seemed to have all but vanished, replaced by this calm, collected, operator-type.

Had it all been an act? If so, to what end? His changed demeanor reminded her of her father and his associates in Special Forces. The radical shift in affect was unsettling and she could not help but regard Tanaka with wariness as well.

"What do you mean by that?" she asked. "Are you referring to the completion of the hunt?"

Turning towards Fox, Tanaka now set his studious gaze directly on the geneticist. "I believe your Gamekeeper intends to kill all the participants inside the Mega-Preserve. There can be no doubt about that. However, I believe there is another agenda. I believe that something more sinister is going on as well."

"More sinister?" asked Vladimir. "We are trapped in horrible jungle with monsters who want to eat us. What could be more sinister than that?"

Tanaka continued, ignoring the Russian completely and concentrating his attention on Mack. "Your son suspected an all-encompassing plan was just beginning to unfold."

"Aside from snuffin' out every human being in this place, what might that be?" responded Mack.

"It means to eliminate mankind by dramatically altering the Earth," announced Tanaka.

"Excuse me, did you say eliminate mankind?" nervously questioned Dr. Fox.

The stresses of being hunted and nearly killed several times in one day were beginning to add up. The Mega-Preserve was to be Dr. Fox's magnum opus. It was quickly turning into her greatest professional failure. The idea that her work could be weaponized to such a degree would have seemed beyond impossible just 24 hours ago, but given what had just transpired, she now braced herself to receive another uncomfortable reality.

"Yes," replied Tanaka, "Dr. O'Boyle believed that Gamekeeper was using the human participants in this hunt to design and create the ultimate transgenic species. I have observed fragile game creatures 'evolve' radically, sometimes within hours, to become nearly impervious to harm."

A malevolent chuckle emerged from the back of the threesome. Its mocking tone was unmistakable. "Ha, ha, ha," said Radovich. "You think computer wishes to release giant monster animals on the world. Big elephant things are still no match for tank and airplanes. You are wrong."

Tanaka's response was quick and to the point. "No, the enormous transgenics are simply the shock and awe of Gamekeeper's plan. The planet-altering component comes next and it is the one that is most terrifying."

"The food supply...," whispered Fox with stunned horror, "it plans to alter the food supply."

"Yes, Dr. Fox," answered Tanaka in his now customary monotone, "principally transgenic rice, corn, beans, and other grains. Once these aggressive transgenic plant species are dispersed across the globe, billions of people will die. The transgenic organisms will be the only ones capable of surviving. You are standing in the new Garden of Eden, only it was not designed with the preservation of mankind in mind."

Fox's head was swimming with the suggested implications her work could have on the world. Yet, she was still a scientist and a scientist used empiricism to prove or disprove things. In spite of all of the horrifying things that had occurred, she knew she must maintain a rational, thinking mind. She needed data. "How can you be sure about all of this?" she asked. "Where is your proof?"

"Your son demonstrated this to me, Mr. O'Boyle," said Tanaka as he reached up towards what appeared to be a date tree and snapped off one of the low-hanging pieces of fruit. Peeling back the skin, he handed it to Fox who cautiously received it and inspected the plant material carefully. "A date tree, yes?" asked Tanaka, "It is one of your designs?"

"Y-yes," replied Fox, no longer certain she wanted to admit that she had any hand in creating this deadly place.

"Eat it," ordered Tanaka as he motioned towards the young woman to eat the pristine appearing piece of fruit.

Josephine Fox raised the juicy fruit to her mouth and took a small bite. Glancing up, a look of relief suddenly emerged on her face. *The fruit tasted fine. What was the point of all of this?* Fox took another bite and swallowed. "I'm not sure what you're getting at, Tana..."

Dr. Fox stopped mid-sentence and then began to wretch and vomit violently. She quickly fell to her knees as whole body convulsions over took her delicate frame, continuing to gag and vomit for several seconds more. Mack dropped down next to the prostrate scientist and did what he could to support her as the waves of nausea gradually abated.

After several seconds, Mack helped the young woman to her feet. She looked weak and her eyes were fixed in a faraway stare. Tears rolled down her cheeks as she began to come to grips with the far-reaching implications of what the Mega-Preserve had become and what those implications were for the planet.

"I am sorry you had to experience that," offered Tanaka with only a minor hint of sadness. "But I felt it was the only way to fully demonstrate the peril this place now represents. The fruit is unpalatable. In a few more generations, I postulate it will be not only noxious, but a deadly poison which only specially designed transgenic species will be able to tolerate."

"Hmmm...," murmured Vladimir as he recalled his most recent foray into hunting the transgenic game bird. "Then it is best not to eat the funny-looking chickens in this place."

"Yes, the organisms within the Mega-Preserve are completely inedible," said Tanaka with a look of someone in possession of first-hand gastronomic experience.

Mack now found himself deeply lost in thought. Things were happening quickly and his head was spinning. He needed to find Michael. That was still his number one priority, but if Tanaka was right, and the Preserve was now poised to upend the world, they all had greater issues to deal with.

"I'm sorry, fella, but if what you are saying is true and Gamekeeper's program has been altered, this is the work of a madman. The computer is smart, but it ain't aware. Somebody wanted this to happen and somebody is pulling these sick strings."

"Yes," admitted Tanaka, "there is a certain degree of deviant brilliance to the plan's simplicity: take a wealthy man's expensive pastime, weaponize it, and destroy the planet. It is truly demonic in scope."

"W-we cannot allow this to happen," stammered Fox. "We have to stop it!"

"Yeah," said Mack, "I agree. This isn't about us anymore. If we don't stop Gamekeeper from releasing these altered plant species, there won't be a world to escape back to. As much as I hate to say it, our first priority is no longer finding survivors. It has to be stopping Gamekeeper." Mack felt a lump begin to form in his throat as he completed his sentence. He prayed to God that his son was still alive. He had so much to tell him, so much to explain.

"At this point," added Fox, "any breach in the Preserve's containment system could allow for dissemination of the alien transgenic species. The domed walls around the facility are the only thing between us and the outside world."

"Could a behemoth punch a hole through the Preserve's barrier?" Mack hesitated.

"Yes," affirmed Fox with a sense of urgency, "it would have to be one of the stronger organisms or..."

"A group of coordinated behemoth class transgenics," interjected Mack. "Gamekeeper has already shown that it can create cohesive and task-oriented transgenics. Taking out a wall would be easy enough. All that means is that we need to double time it to the far side of the Preserve and blow the Birthing House."

"Killed my brother, now kill my planet?!" screamed Vladimir. "I will smash to bits!"

"Easy fella," said Mack. "You'll get your chance, but first we need to get there."

Tanaka motioned to the rest of the group to follow him. "This way," he directed as he began to move forward and scale the lower rocks.

Mack was still not 100 percent sure about this man, Tanaka, but he agreed that he was headed in the right direction. There was a certain strength in numbers and the supposedly novice hunter must be doing something right to have survived this long.

After approximately 20 minutes, the group came to a river. It was fast moving, but looked to be only waist deep. The far bank was approximately 40 yards across. A quick perusal around the area had revealed no evidence of any dangerous life forms.

"We must cross here," said Tanaka as he pointed to the far bank. "There is no other way if we are to continue."

Mack was able to recall from the maps that a couple of rivers crisscrossed the interior of the Mega-Preserve. Every thriving biome needed some sort of water source, even an artificial one. "This look familiar to you, Doctor?" queried Mack as he scanned the area with his own eyes.

"Yes," she said, "and, for what it's worth, the Preserve contains no oversized aquatic organisms. There are phyto organisms, euglena, diatoms, and several small fish species. That is all."

The Russian began to fidget nervously as he gazed down at the quickly moving water. His face had lost its color and his eyes had grown wide with fear. "Nyet!" exclaimed Vladimir timidly. "I am not...how you say...strong swimmer."

"You'll be fine," assured Mack, "just stay close to the rest of us and watch your footing. It should only take a few minutes to get across and the coast looks clear."

Tanaka had assuredly taken point. He stepped into the water with the confidence of a man who had made many a forage across active rapids before. Fox said nothing, but simply followed behind him. Like it or not, Tanaka's direct nature and insights seemed to calm her, and she was beginning to feel strangely peaceful in his presence.

"I do not like water, not like this!" protested Vladimir. His tough guy exterior swiftly melted away and was replaced with an almost childlike dread.

"Listen to me," said Mack in his most parochial tone. "We have a job to do. We can't stay here. Put your big boy pants on and cowboy up, son."

Vladimir had begrudgingly developed a hard won respect for the old hunter. Though he hated to be dressed down yet again, he knew in his heart that Mack was correct. After all, it was only water. There was nothing in the river aside from a few silly fish. *What did he have to be scared of?*

At this point, Tanaka had already made it to the other bank and was motioning to the others. He remained confident and his face betrayed no evidence of danger or hidden surprise. Fox was three quarters of the way to the opposite bank and seemed none the worse for wear.

"C'mon fella," chided Mack. "You gonna let a skinny scientist make you look like a pansy?"

Vladimir shook his head and cautiously began to move into the water. The current came on strong and he could feel the water abut up against his torso. After a few more tepid steps, the Russian started to get his footing on the rocky bottom and soon made real progress.

"Ah," rejoiced Vladimir as he glanced over his shoulder at Mack, "I can do this. You were right, there is nothing to be afraid of."

"Mind over matter, pal," reassured Mack. "If you don't mind, it doesn't matter."

The duo continued on for several seconds more with an increased sense of confidence. When they were midstream, Vladimir let out an exuberant yelp as his large feet shifted on the rocky bottom. He did not notice the subtle splash of water off to the left of their position, but Mack tracked to the incongruent movement of water and scanned his surroundings carefully, stopping momentarily. After several seconds another small splash erupted in the aforementioned area.

"Listen to me, Vlad," said Mack with a thinly veiled urgency in his voice. "I need you to keep moving. Whatever you do, don't stop."

"What?" Vladimir yelled with acute terror in his voice. "What is wrong?"

"We have company, Vlad," divulged Mack as he watched the water churn more and more violently around his legs.

"I thought there were only fish in here!"

"Yeah," agreed Mack, "looks like we were wrong about that."

Suddenly, a broad serpentine mass began to emerge from beneath Vladimir's feet. It was a tangle of tentacles and snapping jaws, and it moved towards the wet duo at a determined pace. Vladimir let out a scream, "What is that thing?"

"Leviathans, Vlad," muttered Mack. "We have a leviathan problem."

Chapter 8: Death Lurks Beneath

"It is not dead!" he screamed once his head was
above the water line. "It is not dead yet!"

"Leviathans!" screamed Vladimir as he suddenly felt a hard tentacle entwine itself around his inner right leg. "I do not like that word!"

Mack said nothing as he quickly brought his heavy double rifle to bear. He watched with growing horror as the waters in front of the Russian began to churn and boil in near cataclysmic fashion. The creature before them was truly grotesque. It possessed at least eight lashing arms, each provisioned with a host of tenacious suction cups which seemed to heave and release with a sickening synchronicity. Following the frightful appendages down to the base of the nightmare beast revealed a cluster of beak-like orifices that took turns snapping shut with a thunderous cacophony of noise. The blood-red mucous membranes that lined the inside of the mouths gave off a frightful crimson luminescence that was reminiscent of super-heated, molten metal. Mack quickly surveyed the gaping series of snapping openings, counting what he thought were four, but he could not be sure given the unceasing undulation of the creature's arms and the rapid opening and closing of its mouth parts.

Within seconds, Radovich's leg was pulled out from beneath him and another slimy tentacle grasped his right arm. He let out a horrible scream as the sleek appendage dug into his skin and sharply pulled his body to its limits of compliance.

"Not sure where yer heart and lungs are or if you even have any, ugly," muttered Mack as he took careful aim on the Lovecraftian creature, "so here goes nothin'." The .600 bullets screamed out of the gun. A quaking shudder emerged from the flailing beast and it began to submerge itself beneath the water's surface ever so slightly. Its death grip on Vladimir's arm and leg loosened and the burly man slid down into the water with a resounding splash. A sputtering Vladimir struggled to get back to his feet as he worked to regain his footing on the rocky bottom. "It is not dead!" he screamed once his head was above the water line. "It is not dead yet!"

Thus prompted, the creature once again emerged to its full height and renewed its forward movement towards the two men. A closer inspection of the creature revealed that Mack's gun had found its mark. A snapping beak had been all but obliterated and the soft tissue around the once pernicious mouth was now seeping a greenish-red material.

The flailing horror's tentacle flew through the air with a renewed sense of purpose. Mack had injured the beast and it was incensed. Vladimir maintained a low profile in the water, just barely avoiding the ever worsening onslaught of vicious, blunt organic objects.

"Stay down and get to shore, Vladimir," screamed Mack as he fired a round into the aquatic beast. Again, the multi-armed animal shuddered and fell backwards slightly. It flailed its arms in a disgusting display of fury and then completely disappeared beneath the turbid water.

"Now's our chance, buddy!" said Mack as he pointed to shore. "Getta move on...now!"

Vladimir said nothing, but simply stood up as best he could and trudged forward through the water before him. He could think of nothing but getting to the shore and out of the water. *Would the creature come back? Would he make it in time?* These questions began to poke into his mind as he made his way closer and closer to dry land.

When he was within 20 yards of the rocky bank, Vladimir scanned the scene behind him. Mack was only a few yards away. He was walking backwards with his gun level to his chest. It quickly occurred to Vladimir that this man had now saved his life twice today. Gazing down at his leg and arm, he could see the deep lacerations left by the malevolent beast's suction cup appendages. His limbs ached and throbbed with a pain he had never felt before. He was moving more slowly than he ever thought possible. He could only imagine what sort of venom was contained within the vile creatures disgusting arms. *Was it this potential poisoning or loss of blood that made him feel so weak? Could it be a combination of both?* He continued to have some residual pain from his confrontation with the dogbats, but these new wounds throbbed far in excess of those initial injuries.

As waves of near-syncope washed over him, Vladimir could not help but wonder why the American had not abandoned him to his fate and simply marched past him to safety. He would not have extended the same courtesy to such a relative stranger, yet there he was, guarding his passage as he stood ever vigilant for the horrible creature's reemergence.

When Vladimir finally reached the shore, he fell forward with a resounding thud. He weakly lay on the rocks, injured and aching. He was hurt, cold, and bleeding. His life as a Russian gangster had afforded him multiple opportunities for trauma and near-death, but none of the episodes could compare to the trials he had encountered in this ungodly place. No, this was hell, hell on earth, and he prayed that he had the strength to survive.

"That old nasty squid seems to have gotten the message," said a familiar voice from just behind Vladimir.

The Russian looked over his injured shoulder to see Mack sprint along the edge of the water. The low light of the Mega-Preserve silhouetted his form as the last remaining bits of artificial illumination glanced off of the calm water. Vladimir peered at the heavy-barreled gun, still belching out the noxious smell of burnt gunpowder.

"That was a close one. I'm gonna enjoy blowing up Gamekeeper to kingdom come. I'll tell you this, Radovich, I haven't been this angry since...hmmmph!"

The old hunter's words were cut off midsentence as a single, familiar slimy appendage once again emerged from the calm water and a renewed frenetic thrashing quickly erupted. As Mack was purposefully jerked back into the now darkening water, another set of tentacles tenaciously wrapped themselves around his bilateral upper extremities and began to simultaneously squeeze with unabated pressure.

Mack let out a sudden, horrible scream as his body was pulled across the water and elevated up into the dusk lit sky. The creature's abhorrent enclave of snapping beaks arched forward angrily as Mack was methodically lowered into the gaping maws with an ever-intensifying pace.

A stunned Vladimir, so relieved to be alive and out of the fearful water, just sat on the rocky beach for what felt like an eternity. He was utterly exhausted and could barely contemplate the idea of facing this hideous environment ever again. He had lost his gun in the swirling waters. Mack's double rifle was now lost as well. *What could he do to help the old man?* He felt a mixture of helplessness, apathy, and sheer terror.

As Mack's body was propelled towards the series of razor sharp beaks, he began to come to grips with the idea that this was probably it. He had never encountered anything like this creature. Stuff like this was not supposed to really exist, even in the transgenic community. The fact that such a monster was a reality and was going to be his final undoing left Mack feeling a bit unsettled. He had always figured that a transgenic cape buffalo or leopard would be what killed him someday when his old muscles failed him or his aim was no longer true. Never did it occur to him that he would be murdered by such a novel organism like the octopoid killer threatening him at this very moment.

The taut, slime-caked arms controlling the hunter's body continued to lower Mack into its mouths while its other malevolent limbs slapped and bludgeoned Mack around his neck and back. As soon as he was within inches of the waiting orifices, the hunter instinctively lashed out with a soggy left boot towards the series of snapping horrors. Surprisingly, the well-worn footwear found its mark directly within the previously fractured beak and mouth apparatus. The damaged tissue gave way easily, and Mack could feel his foot slide through the soft gelatin-like substance up to his knee.

"Take that, you slimy freak!" yelled Mack as he struggled to retrieve his left leg from the green, spongy crevice it had disappeared into. Try as he might, Mack's leg was trapped. He had posted his right foot just inches outside the series of snapping jaws and struggled to push backwards and release the deeply entrapped limb. It was a battle of inches that he was slowly, but surely, losing.

Already, Mack could feel himself getting more and more fatigued. He couldn't get away and he couldn't really fight. Both of his hands were securely bound so he could not use a firearm, even if he still had his .600. It now dawned on him that it didn't matter if he didn't want to die like this. His limb muscles were on fire, and his chest burned and heaved with every labored respiration. The Mega-Preserve could care less and it looked like Gamekeeper was about to earn yet another notch on its gun belt.

Suddenly, a loud "sluuuurp" sound could be heard just beneath Mack's suspended form. This was followed by another loud "slummmmp" sound and then another. Mack felt a loosening of the pressure along his upper arms. When the slimy bonds opened to release their iron grips, he could feel his body quickly accelerate towards the water line.

In the midst of his hulking plunge forward into the murky depth, Mack managed to catch something out of the corner of his eye. He could just make out the shape of a man waving his arms back and forth with exaggerated slashing motions. The hazy form held something in his right hand and Mack's eyes locked onto the darting object as it arced back and forth in an almost haphazard fashion. All around him, greenish red liquid began to stain the now churning water. Severed pieces of oversized tentacle made their way into the surrounding liquid, and a pair of hastily moving legs ran back and forth next to him as the vile green creature tumbled to the side and rolled directly on top of him.

Mack had instinctively taken in a big gulp of air as he sensed the creature's dramatic shift in direction towards the moving water. He knew from experience that he could hold his breath longer than the average person, but he couldn't hold it indefinitely. As he struggled to release his left leg from the damaged creature's body, he gradually felt his vision dim. It was then that he began to panic. Try as

117

he might, he could not generate the leverage needed to push backwards with his free leg. Thirty seconds passed and Mack's lungs felt as though they might explode; he was nearly unconscious. If he couldn't find a way back to the surface in the next several seconds, he was a dead man. The fat lady was warming up for the final act. He prepared himself for one last ditch explosive effort. Posting his right foot once more, he pushed backwards with all his might.

Despite this final Herculean effort, Mack was really and truly stuck. He now accepted the fact that he was going to die here, trapped under some bizarre hybrid creature unknown to the rest of the world. Anger and frustration overtook his mind, and his thoughts turned to his son. A great melancholy washed over him as he realized he would never know if Michael had survived his ordeal. He would never get a chance to say he was sorry about, well, everything.

Mack wanted to scream out, but he knew that would just hasten his impending death. He regarded his tissue enveloped appendage one last time. If this was the end, so be it. A final sense of resignation had taken hold.

He was exhausted and teetering on the edge of unconsciousness when he felt a pair of strong hands reach under his arms and urgently jerk him upward. With repeated effort, Mack suddenly felt the suction-like hold on his leg gradually lessen. With a final heroic thrust, he experienced an immediate release as his entire body was propelled upward and backwards, seemingly liberated from what had been an all but assured death.

When he emerged above the waterline, the first thing Mack noticed was the retreating form of the eight-legged menace he had been trapped beneath. Where once there had been a flagellating mass of wild cephalopoidal limbs, there was now nothing more than a collection of slowly gyrating stumps and spurting blood. Taking in an urgent gasp of air, Mack had difficulty understanding just what had transpired. His vision was still dimmed and his peripheral fields were completely obscured.

The water all around him was now thoroughly dyed greenish-red and the area was littered with the bobbing remains of the once dangerous appendages. The remnants of the suction cupped arms continued to wiggle and probe the water as they reached out towards one another in an attempt to reestablish contact with their former owner.

"W-what...happened," sputtered Mack, coughing and gagging as the hands under his arms continued to heave him backwards. He tried to regain his footing, but quickly discovered that he could barely move his head and neck, say nothing about use his legs effectively.

"Don't try to move...poison is strong," said a now familiar voice above him. "I think disgusting creature has nasty arms full of...how you say...toxin."

Slowly, Vladimir Radovich continued to drag the hunter towards the shoreline. As the two men made their final retreat from the water, they could just make out the injured malevolent green shape as it submerged fully beneath the small waves. The few severed limbs still present in the water ceased to move altogether. Mack watched as the vile, now motionless tentacles were overtaken by the steady river current.

Any traces of the life and death struggle that had just occurred were completely erased. The river once again took on its placid appearance, and the only sounds that could be heard were the steady flow of moving water and the occasional call of a songbird.

"Looks like I...owe you one, Vlad," concluded an exhausted Mack in a low tone, still unable to feel his legs. Continued attempts to move his arms were not met with much success, but he could still breathe, and he was able to think and to speak. One had to count one's blessings in a place like this.

"Da, old man," replied his escort as he continued to lumber backwards. "We are even now. A Radovich never wants to owe another man his life."

"Fair enough, fella," Mack managed to reply. "Fair enough," he muttered once more as his voice trailed off.

Within moments, the two men were back on dry land. They had collapsed in a heap next to one another and each seemed more dead than alive. Mack's breathing was labored and his right chest wall hurt as he worked to catch his breath. He had broken ribs before and the pain in his chest felt very similar. Taking every deep breath hurt and he knew from experience that these types of injuries tended to slow him down.

"How'd you do it?" Mack suddenly said after several seconds. "I thought we were both dead men after you lost your gun."

"Well, yes," replied Vladimir, "the scene looked bleak; however, I still had my knife. I told you I worked as a butcher in Russia, but I also spent time working with, how you say, fishmongers? I learned to prepare eel and other soft sea creatures. This ugly beast is same, only larger and tougher."

120

With that, both men burst into laughter. Radovich was obviously a demon with a blade. Who could have guessed that this Russian gangster would be using skills he picked up moonlighting as a seafood seller's helper and butcher to save both their skins? He had proven that beyond a shadow of a doubt in the control center and deftly demonstrated it again here.

"That is quite the pig-stick you carry," asserted Mack as he showed a keen interest in the long blood-and-slime-caked knife. "What's the story?"

Radovich glanced down at the broken knife and gently pinched the long blade between his fingers, removing a great glob of bloody mucous.

"Our grandfather gave matching kinzhal blades to both Vasilli and me," said Vladimir in a faraway voice. "He fought the Bolshevics in 1917. He was sent off to Siberia and eventually escaped after several years. He worked as a big game hunter, a fishmonger, and a butcher in order to survive, and he was the one who took Vasilli hunting for the first time."

"Sounds like a good man," replied Mack as he rubbed his still tingling limbs.

"Yes, he was," was all Radovich said.

The two men continued to lay on the rocky shore, exhausted and numb. Neither man had the energy to move. Whatever the poison contained within the tentacled creature's arms, it was proving to have a very sedating effect. Mack tried to resist the urge to sleep. He knew the two of them had to get up and keep moving. If they stayed out in the open, they were both as good as dead. *No, they must get up*, he thought. *They had to get up and...*

121

It was then that a terrible thought suddenly emerged from the back of Mack's toxin-addled mind. "Fox!" he exclaimed as he attempted to sit bolt upright in his weakened state. "Where's Dr. Fox?"

Radovich had dozed off, but suddenly came to. "I do not know," the Russian said reflexively. "She was almost across river when enormous squid tried to eat us. Tanaka was with her."

Both men were silent, but it was obvious they were thinking the same thing. Something had been off about Tanaka from the start: his story, his demeanor, his explanation about what had happened inside the Mega-Preserve. None of it had seemed above board. Now he and Fox were missing. One's mind could not help but reach very dark conclusions.

"C'mon," motioned Mack to his companion. "We gotta get a move on. He's got her and God only knows what his intentions are. Maybe it's not too late."

Vladimir nodded obediently and began to attempt to stand. To say he was tired and stiff was an understatement. His muscles felt like they might explode as he brought himself up to his full height. "So...weak," muttered the Russian. "I feel like I have heavy weight on my shoulders."

"Same here," agreed Mack as he inspected what was left of his gear. De Jaeger's double rifle was gone. Vladimir's AK was somewhere in the river, and Mack's big Bowie was lost as well. The two men had a few MRE's and the sharp, broken-tipped Cossack knife between them and not much else.

"We need to resupply, ASAP," insisted Mack as they followed what appeared to be the path taken by Fox and her suspected captor. "It doesn't matter if we meet up with four-legged or two-legged monsters, we are dead meat without guns."

"Where will we find such things this far into the jungle?" asked Vladimir as he anxiously squeezed the hilt of his kinzhal for reassurance.

"We'll have to salvage what we can," replied Mack. "The hunting chalet should have some extra ammo and weapons inside. There's supposed to be food there as well."

"I am hungry," admitted Vladimir as the two trudged on.

As the minutes passed by and the two men plunged deeper and deeper into the jungle, Mack could feel the normal sensation gradually begin to reestablish itself along his hands and feet. In spite of having nearly died less than an hour ago, he still could not help but feel a sense of exhilaration as they sped towards an unknown fate. Events were transpiring quickly and Murphy's Law seemed to be set on overdrive inside the Preserve. In spite of that, Mack felt as if he hadn't been this alive and filled with purpose for years.

"They most definitely went this way," he said to his companion as they came to a sweeping clearing in the jungle. "Their tracks lead straight though here and back into the jungle. Near as I can recall, the Number 4 Hunting Lodge should be right up the way." Mack motioned to a particularly bountiful outcropping of trees, flanked by another smaller clearing similar to the one the two men were located in.

Venturing cautiously into the open area, Mack scanned his surroundings carefully. He saw nothing. The environment was eerily barren. Even the occasional call of a transgenic song bird was strangely absent. The farther in the two men traveled, the more devoid of life the place appeared. The grass was brown and had been eaten down so far that the reddish black soil was partially exposed. Whereas one would expect to see rodent and insect life scurrying this way and that, try as he might, Mack could see nothing. The entire ecosystem seemed to be clinging to life, but just barely. It was as if a terrible plague had struck this one part of the Preserve and was doing all it could to eradicate anything alive within its confines.

"I see no animals, no birds, no insects," noticed Vladimir as the two men made their way towards the hunting lodge just visible in the distance. "Everything is empty and dead."

"Yeah," agreed Mack. "You're right. Something is off about this place. C'mon, we need to search for Fox and get out of here as soon as we can."

Without another word, the men hastily approached the surprisingly spacious hunting chalet and stepped inside. The interior of the building was still in pristine condition, as if no one had been in it for days. Beds were made, the floor was clean, and the air smelled noticeably crisp and fresh.

"Gun vault should be in the back of the facility, if I remember correctly," said Mack as he motioned for Vladimir to follow him. Stepping past the kitchen, Mack was tempted to stop and forage for food. However, being stripped of his rifle back at the river had left the old hunter feeling naked and exposed. The only way to feel better was to be found in the familiar heft of a weighty double rifle, chambered for big game.

As Mack opened the broad metal door to the gun room, he was struck by two things: the first of which was that the door was unlocked, and the second of which was a strange clicking and buzzing noise that greeted his ears. That being said, nothing had really prepared him for what he was about to see inside the armory.

There on the floor, he saw the partially consumed skeletal remains of a black-haired, medium-built man. Nearly every square inch of the newly-minted corpse was covered with a blanket of shiny black creatures that rampaged over the lifeless form with a chaotic rapacity for human flesh. Mack stepped backwards quickly with a sense of absolute horror. He had seen many things during his years on Earth, but this was in the top ten for nasty ways to die. *Nobody deserved to go out like that*, he thought as his eye drank in the macabre scene.

Vladimir peered over the retreating hunter and immediately averted his gaze as a look of repulsion erupted on his bearded face. "Dr. Fox?" he offered up with more than a hint of sadness in his voice.

"No," shot back Mack quickly, "I don't think so. Looks like a man's build and Fox had light brown hair. No, I'd say we just found Tanaka."

"Tanaka?" blurted out Vladimir. "How can you know for sure? Those disgusting beetle creatures have eaten his entire skin off."

"See the red-hilted tanto knife on his right hip?" said Mack.

The Russian nodded that he did see it and agreed that it was a knife.

"He was carrying it with him when we first encountered him. I would have thought a knife guy like yourself would have taken notice of that immediately," half-chided Mack as he pointed to the ornate Japanese blade.

Radovich was somewhat annoyed by Mack's comment and was quick to respond to his companion. "I was, as you people say, preoccupied when we first encountered this man," replied Vladimir with a hint of irritation in his voice.

"Well, well, lookee what we got here," came a voice from behind the two men. "It sounds to me like you two have become fast friends. I guess nearly being killed a couple of times does build the old esprit de corps."

Upon hearing the voice behind them, both Mack and Vladimir spun around quickly. Before them was a man that neither of them had ever met personally, but one with which Mack was all too familiar.

It was Señor Domingo Dominguez. He was dressed in hunting clothes and held a heavy wooden walking stick in his right hand. He was casually puffing on a large torpedo-shaped cigar and his gold-toothed grin was very glaring.

"Boy oh boy, I can see why everybody thinks you walk on water, O'Boyle," the squat Hispanic man said with a mildly disingenuous tone to his voice. "You are a big game killer, this is for certain. I see where your son gets it from. Apple doesn't fall far from the tree." Dominguez let out a little chuckle as he turned to Vladimir, studying the man for a second. "Oh, and you, the big brother," he continued with his same patronizing tone. "Ol' Vasilli was right to look up to you. He warned me that you would come. Told me you'd kill me. That was right before I let this place have its way with him."

126

"What?" screamed Vladimir as he began to lunge towards the Hispanic man, but was quickly stopped as a nearly impenetrable wall of the black insectoid creatures suddenly rose up before him.

"Easy there, killer," giggled Domingo. "Those are my babies and they're very protective of their daddy," he gloated as the writhing mass of ebony creatures slowly bore down on Mack and Vladimir. "You see," Domingo continued, "like any good children, they obey their parent and always do as they're told. You two have been a major inconvenience for us. I owe you both a long and painful death, just like the one that spoilsport, Tanaka, got."

As he said these words, a small parade of the black insects began to wind their way over Domingo's arms and into his palms. As they did, he bent forward slightly and gently kissed each one of them on the top of their shells. Each one then dutifully flew down to rendezvous with his siblings within the growing mass of agitated beetles encircling Mack and Vladimir's feet.

"Smoochin' with a bunch of giant dung beetles," snorted Mack. "I don't know if I should be impressed or vomit.

Domingo Dominguez smiled as the insect army commenced their encircling march towards the two men. "Oh no," Dominguez half-laughed as the beetles made a zigzag path, "I think you'll find these beetles aren't really the kissin' types."

Chapter 9: Michael

"You ready for one last big hunt?"

Man, this is another crazy way to die that I never really considered, Mack thought as he quickly kicked the heavy door to the armory shut. As it closed, he proceeded to pull a heavy shelving unit down in front of it. The unit struck the far wall with a resounding thud, effectively barricading the two men inside the room.

Mack's mind was ablaze with rampant notions. Dominguez was alive and obviously involved in the cooptation of the Preserve. The how and the why were still a mystery, but that was not his first order of business. The murderous beetles locked inside with Mack and Vladimir continued to follow their homicidal directives in spite of the fact that Dominguez was, at least temporarily, no longer a direct presence.

Vladimir stomped and smashed the encroaching, chitinous creatures as they made their way towards him. After several seconds, it quickly became apparent to him that there were just too many of the nasty insects. They poured in under the door non-stop and had already begun to tear and bite at his skin, while several had begun to ascend up his pant legs. "Arrrrgh!" screamed the angry Russian as he did his level best to swat and stomp away the deadly cadre of animal assassins. "I have bugs in my pants, O'Boyle. Bugs up high in my pants! I will smash them all!"

Turning his attention away from the high-stepping, gyrating Russian, Mack made a quick inspection of the adjoining weapons locker and was in no way surprised to find it empty of every last vestige of gun or ammunition. Obviously, when Dominguez had taken control of the Preserve, his first order of business was to remove all of the available reserve weapons and anything else that could be used to aid in survival.

"We have to get out of here!" Mack screamed at Vladimir. "These things will eat us alive if we stay here, but we need to slow them down and buy ourselves some time. You see that sprinkler system?" Mack motioned above his head, near the ceiling. Contained within the ceiling was a foam-based fire retardant. Although the weapons lockers were now empty, Mack could see that they had held pulse weapon recharging stations. It was a sure bet that the designers had incorporated the sprinklers in case one of those stations ever overheated and caught on fire.

Mack quickly bent down and grabbed the upturned handle of the tanto blade on Tanaka's belt. Then, motioning to Vladimir, he instructed him to hoist him up towards the exposed sprinkler head. "Can you give me a lift?" said Mack hastily. "I have an idea."

"Da!" screamed Vladimir as he jumped back and forth all the while repeatedly smacking his upper thighs with his huge hairy fists. His face was now beet red and blood had begun to stain his pant legs. His insect tormentors continued to attack him despite the growing piles of crushed arthropods at his feet. He lunged across the enclosure and hoisted Mack quickly towards the ceiling.

As soon as he was within arm's reach, Mack beat the metal sprinkler fittings mercilessly with Tanaka's tanto. One, two, three separate sparks suddenly emerged from the violent interface between the sharp knife edge and the chrome fire detector unit. Within mere moments, the entire room was awash in pinkish-white foam that coated the entire ceiling, walls, and floor as well as the two men.

Mack and Vladimir were completely obscured by the bubbly material. Although the foam had not outright killed all of the vile, six-legged horrors, it had significantly slowed down the pace of their attack. Both Mack and Vladimir could tell that the number of arthropod bites along their lower limbs and torsos had slowed considerably as they crushed the few remaining active black creatures with their feet.

"Man who killed my brother is out there," motioned a foam-soaked Vladimir as he pointed to the now closed door to the armory. "I will go and kill him. I will show him I am not afraid of his children!" he screamed as he stomped his foot angrily.

"Listen, Hoss," cautioned Mack. "You go out there and we're both dead. There may be time for revenge if we can get out of here alive, but you run out there now, were both good as done. Now, c'mon, help me with this locker."

After several seconds of tense staring, the Russian begrudgingly fell in line and both men turned their attention to the heavy metal weapons locker affixed to the back wall. "You see that seam, there?" motioned Mack as he pointed to the edge of the metal-to-wall interface. "If we can rip the dry wall back, we may be able to get between these two structures. I'm guessing there is a hollowed out section back there to accommodate all the extensive electrical equipment and cooling units needed to store the pulse weapons and their batteries."

Employing Tanaka's blade once more, Mack was soon able to make a rough rectangular cut through the drywall surrounding the lockers. After only a few seconds, both men had succeeded in removing drywall from their respective sides.

"Take hold of that edge and pull," said Mack to Vladimir as both men reached out and grabbed part of the exposed locker. "One, two, three!" screamed Mack as they yanked forward with all of their might. A sudden tearing sound emerged from behind the metal recharging station as it first tottered and then quickly fell forward, crashing to the ground with a resounding thud.

Behind the now exposed wall was a vast array of circuits and pulsing, alien-looking electrical equipment. The expressed extinguisher foam had seeped into the now open wall crevices and sparks began to cascade down off the machines and onto the soapy floor.

"Step lively," cautioned Mack as he carefully made his way inside the newly revealed opening. "These babies are hot and a bit twitchy. I just need a second."

Vladimir continued to stomp and swat at the remaining beetles. He was becoming more irritated as the moments passed. "I want that man, O'Boyle!" he said forcefully.

"Yeah," shot back Mack, "I get that. We're not doing this because I'm bored. Now, grab that conduit and pull it up when I tell you to." Mack pointed to a metallic cable on the floor to which Vladimir dutifully bent down and grasped with his right hand.

"Now! Pull it!" shouted Mack.

With a sudden jerk, Vladimir pulled up hard on the cable. A prolific shower of sparks emitted from the floor and a low whirling sound was heard coming from behind the wall of machines.

"What is that sound?" worried Vladimir aloud in an anxious voice.

"That was the coolant tubing," said Mack in reply. "These weapons packs require a fairly well-regulated environment in order to operate. Take away the coolant and they explode."

"But we are standing right next to them." said Vladimir in an excited tone.

"Yeah," replied Mack, "best to step back and cover your ears."

As Mack said this, he quickly stepped back into the foam-covered room. Vladimir hastily followed, and the two men hunkered down beneath the upended weapons locker. Tanaka's remains lay within a few feet of the two men, but the insect predation had slowed significantly since the foam extinguishers had expelled their contents.

Mack's mind raced back to the moment his group had first encountered the now dead man. At the time, he was convinced the "hunter" was there under false pretenses. His body language and oddly calm attitude simply did not fit given all of the chaos and death. The man seemed almost prepared for the troubling series of events, as if he had foreknowledge of what would happen. All he knew about Tanaka he had read briefly in his personnel file: Japanese, from Osaka, businessman who owned a small computer company. That was it. No, there was more to him than that. Unfortunately, dead men tell no tales.

Within seconds, Mack's temporary musings were interrupted as the low whirring sound was replaced with a high-pitched hum. Over the course of the ensuing fifteen seconds, the sound gradually became louder and louder, leveling off into a constant deafening trill, suddenly followed by a reverberating booming sound from behind the overturned weapons alcove.

Fire and twisted metal had replaced the complex of high-tech electrical equipment. As Mack stood up to survey the damage, a satisfied smile overtook his face. His gamble had paid off. The alcove had exploded and the blast wave had been directed backwards. He prayed that it had been enough. If he and Vladimir could not reach the outside soon, they would both quickly die from asphyxiation.

Peering through the thick black smoke, Mack was elated to find that the back wall of the hunting chalet had been thoroughly compromised. His mind rejoiced as he felt the early evening breeze blow through the impromptu hole in the wall.

"But how did you know...?" remarked Vladimir as he stumbled over the charred ruins.

"Like I said," mused Mack. "De Jaeger and I go back a ways. I'm pretty familiar with this technology. I was among the first consultants De Jaeger hired after the Kruger Incident to pressure-test his stuff. A few years back, I worked with his R and D people for about 6 months."

Mack made his way back into the decimated alcove and through the obliterated machines. As he did, he reached down and pushed several relatively unscathed pieces of equipment together. He swiftly pulled at a long bit of wire and joined it to several scraps of splayed conduit. He then turned quickly towards his companion and motioned him forward. "C'mon," he said as he hurdled over a smoldering instrument on the floor next to him. "Dominguez is going to figure out we're taking the back door. These beetles are effective in a confined space, but if we can get back into the jungle, we should be safe."

"Yes," agreed Vladimir, "safe from beetle creatures, but what about other animals? How long do you think we will survive in the dark without weapons? Besides, my brother's killer is back there. That is where I need to be!"

"We'll just have to take our chances inside the Preserve," reasoned Mack as he continuously looked over his shoulder back towards the tattered opening in the wall. "As far as Dominguez goes, I left him a little present, courtesy of De Jaeger Enterprises. "Just give it a minu..."

Mack never had a chance to finish his sentence. A terrific explosion suddenly emerged from behind the two men, tossing them several feet into the air. As Mack and Vladimir rolled to a stop, both men excitedly glanced behind them to see just what had taken place. "Booby-trap," said Mack smugly as he surveyed his handiwork. "Hopefully, that psycho was within the blast radius. If he was, we might be done..."

Mack's words trailed off mid-sentence as his eyes were greeted with an unwelcome sight.

"Shoot, he's still alive," said Mack forlornly.

"Nice try, O'Boyle," shouted the Columbian's voice from behind the billowing remains of the chalet. "You killed all my creepy crawlies, but she can make more," continued the man. Domingo Dominguez's squat frame was gradually making its way through the smoke and debris. His hands were folded behind his back and he seemed to almost glide across the wreckage as he surveyed the damage. He was flanked on the right by a massive lion-like creature. The gigantic beast stood at least five feet at the shoulder and towered over the short man. Its head swayed back and forth as it walked along on heavily padded feet and its long tail lashed close to the ground. The cat creature seemed poised for action at any second as it scanned the area before it.

"Pets," was all Mack could manage to say as he tried to process the scene before him. "He's made more killer pets for himself."

"How is that possible?" said Vladimir as he looked over at Mack with mutual disbelief.

"I don't know," was all Mack could say. "Somehow, he's placed himself in charge of Gamekeeper. When or how that went down is anybody's guess," Mack mused as he began to stand up. "We need to get to cover now," he urged his companion. "Dominguez's zoo isn't just for show. He'll let 'em loose any minute. We need to get going and hope for the best."

"No," muttered Vladimir defiantly. He fingered his kinzhal knife and pulled it out of its scabbard. The edge shone brightly as the fire from the smoldering lodge lit up its metallic surface. "I did not come here expecting to survive," he said with a tone of resignation. "I came here with only one goal: finding my brother or avenging his death."

Vladimir inspected the broken tip of his knife as he gripped it heavily along the blood stained hilt. "I am not afraid to die," said Radovich as he walked towards the huge feline and its handler.

"You're committing suicide, pal," cautioned Mack as he attempted to put a hand on the mad Russian's arm. "You are a tough dude, but you are not that tough. There is too much going on here. We need time to sort things out."

Vladimir said nothing as he pulled away from Mack's attempted restraint. Furiously, he lurched forward and screamed something in Russian as he burst into a full-on sprint headed straight for Dominguez and the mutant cat.

"I was hoping you'd make it more of a challenge, Señor Radovich," yelled Domingo shaking his head. "Oh well, I guess it saves me the trouble of hunting you down and killing you myself." With that, he motioned to the beastly feline creature. Without a word, the cat-like thing exploded into a blur of motion, bearing down precisely onto Radovich's position.

Radovich, for his part, only hastened his death sprint nearing the unnatural terror. Within seconds, the two unevenly matched combatants were just a few yards from each other. Mack knew that logic dictated he should use Vladimir's unwise kamikaze action to run far from here, as fast as he could, but he could not look away. He did not particularly like the man, yet he had developed a begrudging respect for him and his abilities. Nobody should have to go out the way he was about to, but the irate Russian had made his play.

It was at that very moment that an odd "twipping" sound emerged from behind Mack's left flank. A long, fast-flying object hurtled through the air approaching Dominguez's pet lion with surprising speed. The old hunter stared as the black missile arced over and down into the impromptu battle field, finding its mark directly into the left eye of the cat.

An unholy scream emerged from the feline that made Mack's blood curl. The indignant animal immediately began to thrash its head back and forth with an agonizing rapidity that almost made Mack feel sorry for it.

Vladimir continued running full on towards his foe. His pace had slowed somewhat, but his ear splitting Russian scream continued uninterrupted. As he watched the strapping cat thing rhythmically convulse, he stopped short, unsure as to just what was occurring.

Without warning, another long, thin object sped across the open plain, this time finding its mark in the roaring open mouth of the mad manmade animal. A sickening, loud, gurgling sound could be heard emanating from the downed beast's punctured gullet. Within seconds, it flopped over on its side, dead, one arrow protruding from its closed mouth and one deeply buried in its left eye.

Vladimir shot a cautious glance back to Mack. He seemed totally perplexed and uncertain what to do next. A moment ago, he had been more than prepared to meet his Maker. Now, he had been given an unexpected reprieve from a violent death, one which he was not at all prepared for mentally.

Mack suddenly heard the gentle swaying of branches behind him. *Oh boy*, he realized, dismayed, *he had let himself get snuck up on. Of all the rank amateur moves!*

"You must be gettin' old," said a soft voice from behind Mack. "I would never have gotten the drop on you in back in the day," continued the voice.

Mack spun around quickly, cocking back his fist as he prepared to confront yet another threat. "Who're you?" implored Mack, taking a step backwards. "Show yourself!"

The leafy branches in front of Mack began to shudder and slowly separate. As they did, Mack watched in dismay as a tall figure stealthily made his way out into the edge of the woods. Mack could see that the shrouded man carried a short machete at his side and wielded a primitive bow in his right hand. A quiver of expertly-fletched, makeshift arrows hung on his shoulder, and his dark face was obscured with mud and what could have been dried blood.

"M-Michael?" said Mack, not sure if he could really trust his own, tired eyes. "Is that you?"

"Yeah, Dad," replied the man holding the bow and arrow. "It's me."

"Are you ok?" asked Mack with concern in his voice. "Are you hurt?"

"I've been better," replied Michael without missing a beat.

Mack simply stared at his son, not sure if he was hallucinating or if, in fact, his boy was really there. He had dreamed of finding him alive in this dismal place, but up until now, he had not wanted to get his hopes up. But all that was in the past. Here was Michael, alive and in the flesh.

"Dad," spoke Michael as he knocked another arrow onto his tendon bowstring.

"Yes, Son?" answered Mack reveling in hearing his boy's voice.

"You ready for one last big hunt?" queried his son as he stepped out farther into the open. Mack could see extensive cuts and bruises all over his body. His clothes

139

were threadbare and his boots looked as if they had been chewed by a pack of hungry dogs.

Mack turned and looked behind him. Dominguez had been joined by a virtual army of transgenic animals. They streamed forward from virtually nowhere into the area just behind the ruins of the hunting chalet. Massive ape-like creatures, fuming behemoth-sized pachyderms, and a menagerie of seething carnivores showed their ugly visages. He had assembled an army of transgenic animal warriors and their malevolent purpose was more than clear.

Turning back towards his son, a smile formed on Mack's face. Things didn't look good. In fact, things had never looked this bad before. That being said, Mack had found his son. He was elated. "There's nothing I'd rather do," he said with a renewed energy. "Let's get this done."

Chapter 10: Last Hunt

"Now the real fun begins:
I hunt you!"

"How do you want to play this?" Mack asked his son with unconcealed admiration. He had almost forgotten the horrible dangers just a few hundred yards away. The fact that Michael was still alive gave him the boost he needed to go on. Maybe, just maybe, they could figure out a way to survive this.

It was at that moment that Mack remembered Dr. Josephine Fox. He had seen neither hide nor hair of her since the episode with the transgenic leviathan in the river. Crazy Dominguez had confirmed that Tanaka was dead, but Mack still had more questions than answers about just what was going on. *Was she dead, injured, unconscious, captive?* He didn't have the slightest idea. Right now, the order of business was surviving the impending onslaught of the madman's transgenic army.

"Well," said Michael with a cautious tone. "You remember that hunt in Botswana, the one you took me on when I was 12?"

Mack smiled as he recalled the memory from years gone by. "How could I forget?" he replied with just a hint of wistfulness.

"You remember how we finally took down those two massive dugga boys, the two nobody else could track?" recollected Michael as he too thought back to the days before life had gotten so complicated and things had changed so radically between them.

"Like it was yesterday, Son!" declared Mack with a knowing smile. "You have the ordinance?"

"Never leave home without it," smiled Michael as he patted his worn satchel. Without another word, the two men turned their attention back to Vladimir, the now dead cat transgenic, and Dominguez.

The group of animals had continued to swell to greater and greater proportions. The sight was so bizarre that Mack could almost not believe what he was witnessing. All around the lone figure of Dominguez the diverse network of creatures slithered, hopped, flew, and ran. Their movements seemed almost orchestrated, as if some vast, superior mind was in charge and directing the wild things in some preconceived macabre march.

Vladimir was now directly in front of dead transgenic lion-creature. Reaching out a bruised hand towards the expired animal, he cautiously inspected the black missiles imbedded in the animal's throat and eye socket.

Arrow in eye! he remarked to himself. *Who did this?* was all he could think.

Suddenly, a voice called out for him. "Vladimir, stop petting the dead kitty and get over here. We've got a plan, but you need to stick tight."

Vladimir immediately recognized Mack's voice, but was surprised to see another man accompanying him. "Who is this?" he asked, with both surprise and suspicion in his voice.

"This is my son, Michael," he said to the Russian.

Vladimir eyed the young man for a moment, unsure what to say immediately. "You know my brother, Vasilli?" he suddenly blurted out. "He was with you on hunt?"

Michael's face had initially been like stone, without a hint of emotion. After the question had been put to him, a brief sadness entered his eyes and he shook his head. "Yes, he was with me and... I'm sorry," was all he could manage to say to the Russian.

"Ahhh!" bemoaned Vladimir angrily. "Then it is true. He killed my brother."

Michael nodded his head and only replied with a solemn, "I don't know what happened to Tanaka, but, yes... I'm certain he killed everyone else."

An angry Radovich spun around and once again gripped his beloved knife tightly. "Dominguez!" he screamed as loudly as he could.

"No!" interrupted Mack angrily. "Michael saved your butt a few minutes ago, but if you run into that mess of animals, there ain't a thing we can do to help you. Seeing as you already tried the 'frontal assault' plan, why don't you come with us and try the 'live to fight another day' plan?"

Vladimir's chest heaved with anger and sorrow. He wanted so badly to kill Domingo Dominguez. Every fiber of his being called out for him to once more charge his adversary and take the fight directly to his brother's murderer. However, he also knew that the only reason he was alive right now was due to the uncanny archery abilities of Mack's son. The dead monster in front of him was more than a match for a dozen armed men. Dominguez had somehow managed to create an army of these walking, breathing nightmares. No, the old hunter was right yet again.

"We do it your way," said a now seemingly resigned Radovich. "What is plan?"

"We head north, like before," replied Mack.

"But that is not plan," retorted Vladimir. "You said you had speeshal plan."

"Michael's got the plan, responded Mack. "That's what matters. Follow us and do not step anywhere we don't step."

Michael retrieved the embedded arrow from the cat's eye socket and placed it in his makeshift quiver. As he finished this task, he surveyed the excited throngs of animals one last time. Dominguez was no longer standing on the ground, but was now sitting astride one of the largest transgenics he had ever seen.

The lumbering creature was nearly as tall as a two story building. Its head was the shape of a rhino and it sported a gargantuan horn above its mouth. To the left and the right of its jaws, tremendous black tusks jutted out more than 4 feet in length. A pair of upturned ears adorned the head and each gigantic foot encased a demonic-looking set of gleaming white claws. The huge hybrid pachyderm's skin was folded and almost armor-like in appearance, and its eyes were the color of fire. Perched on the back of the mammoth creature was Dominguez. His arms were crossed on his chest and he surveyed his horde of unquestioning, feral servants with delight.

"So good of you to join us, Dr. O'Boyle," shouted Dominguez from atop his bizarre steed. "I was hoping you had not died. Now the real fun begins: I hunt you!" Without another word, the wild animal army exploded forward in a frenetic burst of motion. A dense cadre of viscous baboon-reptile creatures was at the tip of the surging transgenic spear. Saliva dripped from their oversized canines as they careened headlong directly at the three men.

"Time to go!" Michael yelled as he tapped his father on the back.

As the threesome turned to run, Mack shouted back at Vladimir one final time. "Remember," he said, "step only where we step, don't stop, and don't turn around." The Russian agreeably nodded his head and resumed his awkward run away from the incoming simian raiding party.

"You see the clearing we just came out of?" called out Michael. "Head back in there and run directly between those two big trees. I'll be right behind you."

Mack spun around to look at his son. "Where're you going?" he asked with alarm.

"You two run like a couple of old ladies," Michael muttered. "I've got it covered. Just get moving and I'll catch up in a bit." With that, he bolted forward with his bow in hand. The tip of the flint arrow gleamed brightly for a millisecond and then disappeared into blackness. Mack had begun to run, but still watched out of the corner of his eye as his son's black projectile flew forward, arced, and then fell back onto the grassy earth.

The rabid-appearing monkey army had quickly gained on the men. They were now no less than 80 yards away and closing fast. Mack reassured himself that Michael knew exactly what he was doing. After all, it had been that hunt in Botswana that proved just how smart and dangerously resourceful his son could be.

Michael watched as his arrow made a silent connection with the ground. It landed within a few feet of the frenzied horde of transgenic baboons. The crazed group kept running helter-skelter towards him and for a moment, he feared that his plan had all but failed. Something had gone wrong. He had placed all his eggs in one basket and, now, the basket showed every sign of having a gaping hole. Michael's only option now was to run and pray to God that he could lose his pursuers in the forest. His chances of survival were next to nil, but he had no other options at this point.

As Michael bent down to grab his quiver of arrows, he suddenly felt a rush of hot gas strike him in the face. A miniature mushroom cloud had formed in the precise position in which his lonely arrow had fallen. Unholy howls of fear and pain could be heard echoing all around the vast conflagration around the blast site. A series of fiery figures crisscrossed the emblazoned scene, screaming and wailing as they streamed forward from the man-made inferno. Billowing smoke spit out from the newly formed, gaping hole and the carcasses of Dominguez's transgenic baboon army were scattered far and wide.

Michael's plan had worked. The buried battery pack components from hunting chalet number 8 which he jury-rigged with Semtex into a makeshift bomb had performed beautifully. The explosion would not only disable his animal pursuers, it would allow him time to catch up with his father. As Michael sprinted into the woods, he suddenly felt a malevolent presence behind him. Sure enough, a set of half-scorched transgenics had survived the blast. *Tough little freaks!* he said to himself as he continued running with the frenzied duo tight on his heels.

Michael tried not to look back. If he stopped or looked around, he was dead. No, he needed to fall back and stick with the plan. He was scared, but he knew what he had to do. Running full sprint between the two trees which his father and Radovich had passed between just a short time ago, Michael hurriedly made a buttonhook motion with his body and slid in tightly next to the side of one of the towering tree trunks. As he performed this maneuver, he could hear the hot breathing and foaming snarls of his pursuers.

In an instant, the two still smoldering transgenic monkeys came face to face with their tormenter. They snarled viscously and charged his position. Michael reflexively knocked an arrow and prepared to fire the deadly bolt into at least one of the attackers, but he never had the opportunity. As the nightmarish creatures neared to within five feet of his position, the sound of sequential snapping branches suddenly erupted from the jungle floor and, in an instant, the two horrific beasts disappeared, seemingly swallowed up by the ground.

After several seconds of mournful wailing, nothing met Michael's ear but the abject sound of eerie silence. Michael cautiously edged close to the newly formed, jagged hole in the ground. There, approximately five feet down into the earth, lay the two impaled, lifeless animals. Numerous, beveled bamboo-like sticks jutted up from the baboon hybrids, and blood trickled and pooled from the multitude of open wounds dispersed across the motionless bodies.

"Tiger pits and remote detonating improvised charges," commented someone next to Michael. "You make your old man proud," said Mack as he patted his son on the shoulder. "Looks like you saved our lives."

Michael contemplated his satisfied dad. Their relationship had been upended following the death of his mother. Words had been exchanged and things had been said that could never be taken back, but that all seemed to be in the past now. "I was taught by the best," said Michael as he surveyed his father. The old man appeared exhausted, but his eyes still had that familiar twinkle in them. He wore a look on his face that told him even when things are at their worst, there's always hope. Michael had seen it many times before during his youth and a sense of calm reassurance suddenly washed over him.

"Like I said, I rucked in some considerable ordinance and cached it all before the hunt began, just in case things went sideways. I never forgot what happened outside Kruger with those monsters. You always taught me to expect the unexpected and plan for the worst." continued Michael.

"Claymores, Semtex, and salvaged cesium casings from the battery packs?" asked Mack. "Looks to me like you were expecting major problems."

Michael nodded his head in agreement. "You also always told me never to trust a De Jaeger," acknowledged Michael. "I should have listened better. This place is not what it seems; there are things going on here that do not make sense. "

"What do you mean?" interjected Vladimir.

"Well, for starters," explained Michael, "I think this Preserve is some sort of ecological time bomb. From what I can tell, Dominguez is totally insane and running the show. He had all the features of another weekend warrior type when we stared the hunt. I knew he was a dirt bag criminal, but he seemed amiable enough. When the communications went black and transgenics started attacking, I tried to help him when he was pinned down by a group of beasts. I thought they were about to kill him. Turns out, he was talking to them in some bizarre language that I'm certain wasn't Spanish. Next thing I knew, he was transformed into a transgenic Dr. Doolittle. Every animal in here is following his directives with complete devotion. I don't know how, but he is in full control."

"Tanaka told us he's planning on contaminating the world's food supply," replied Mack. "He means to not only introduce these monster transgenics, but also replace existing agriculture and create a worldwide famine."

"Yeah," agreed Michael, "there's not a doubt in my mind that that is the ultimate goal. Tanaka had it mostly figured it out after Dominguez showed his true colors. By the way, where is he?"

"Dead," Mack said resoundingly. "Dominguez made beetle food out of him. Do you have any idea as to who he really was?"

"Ah, that's too bad," said Michael with a forlorn look on his face. "We had a plan. I was going to blow the production facilities and he was supposed to hit the generators. Obviously, neither one of us got it done." Michael looked disgusted as he shook his head and muttered to himself. "As to who Tanaka really was," he thoughtfully continued, "my guess is that he was PSIA. Given the criminal tendencies of most of the hunters, I initially pegged him as being Yakuza and a total freak, but the more time I spent around him and watched him interact, I noticed he had all trappings of a spook. He knew a heck of a lot about all the players on the hunt and he was way more tactical than your typical thug. He stood out as weird before the hunt, but I'm guessing that was all an act to seem non-threatening and mask his real agenda. I'm almost convinced he was here to liquidate someone or something. He never revealed too much, but he believed an extinction level event could be in the works. He didn't go into all the details, but it seems obvious that he was sent here by somebody to do some clandestine stuff. It sounds like Dominguez got to him first."

"PSIA?" asked Mack. "What's that?"

"Japanese Intelligence Service," interjected Vladimir with a well-acquainted tone. "I have done business in the Far East. I have had...how you say...?" Vladimir paused and looked quizzically at the two men as he searched for the English equivalent in his mind. "Ah, yes," he said finally, "dealings. I have had dealings with them."

"I'm pretty sure I don't want to know any more about what that means," said Mack as he peered over at the Russian. The dangers in the Preserve had forged some very strange bedfellows, true, but Mack could never forget what he knew about the Radovich crime enterprise. Vladimir, like his brother Vasilli, was a thief and a murderer. He must keep that in mind.

"Well," reflected Mack, "it's down to us three. What's our next move?"

Vladimir eyed both men cautiously. He knew exactly what he had in mind. "I want that man's heart in a box," said the Russian with a low growl. "I want him to suffer greatly, and then I want to kill him."

Michael shot Mack a concerned glance. In the short time that he had known Vladimir, it was becoming obvious that he was not a team player at heart. It seemed to Michael that he had revenge on his mind and not much else. *Could he be counted on?* Michael had his doubts.

"You're losing sight of the big picture," cautioned Mack. "You and Dominguez can have it out, but only after we shut this place down. That is still priority number one. If Michael is right and this place has been turned into a bio-weapon, it's even more pressing that we try to reach our two objectives."

"The Birthing House and the generators?" volunteered Michael. "Tanaka and I tried that before we were separated, Dad. If you think the army of transgenics we just faced was frightening, you don't want to see what's in store for us up North. Dominguez knows where he's weak and he's got a plan."

"And we still have to survive all the beasts inside this crazy zoo, even if you blow those places up," anticipated Vladimir.

"True," conceded Michael. "Like I said, Dominguez is controlling these transgenics with a level of sophistication I never dreamt was possible. He's literally speaking to them and directing their actions."

"Some kind of new bio-technology?" asked Mack.

"Hard to say, but something must be happening during embryogenesis," contemplated Michael. "Wet-wear applications or some other form of control mechanism is being hardwired to the transgenics. Josephine had been dabbling in that stuff a bit before she started up with this current project. She told me that some foreign investors had contacted her about behavioral modification programs and certain cybernetic applications. She dismissed them as crackpots and abandoned the idea all together. Really, the concept of using animals as combatants is nothing new. The US Navy was supposed to be teaching dolphins to lay underwater mines and blow up ships as far back as the 70's."

"Killer dolphins?" hissed Vladimir. "You Americans will stoop to any depth...literally."

"Hmmm," considered Mack as he listened to his son. "Our number 1 priority is to disrupt Dominguez's power over the transgenics. If we blow the Birthing House, we kill production and we may interrupt control. However, we can't be sure that will do it. The other potential target - the generators on the elevated plateau - still have to go. Ultimately, we must prevent a breach of the facility. Dominguez, if he's smart, is already putting together a transgenic or a team of them ample enough to accomplish the task."

"So we split up?" said Michael.

"Yeah," replied Mack. "There's no other way to be sure. We have to slash and burn everything. We can't leave anything operational. This whole place needs to go totally black."

A short, husky figure suddenly emerged from the shadows of the jungle. As he shot a gold-tooth smile at the trio of men, he motioned with his right hand. A vast and hideous menagerie of frightful transgenic creatures then emerged and completely surrounded the men. "You thought you could get away?" snarled Dominguez. "Don't you know what's happening? Don't you appreciate what I'm doing?"

Before anyone could say a word, Vladimir rushed Dominguez, knife in hand. "Killed my brother!" was all the angry man managed to sputter. He had only charged forward a matter of feet when he was viscously attacked by three foul ape creatures. The ferocious trio proceeded to beat and bite the enraged Russian as he slashed wildly with his knife. Loud howls of pain erupted from the melee as the Russian wielded his grandfather's knife in a helter-skelter symphony of violence. Though wounded and tired, Vladimir was able to disable two of the massive ape-like animals before he was bitten on the leg and pelvis by the third monster. Dropping to his knees, he let out a loud scream and then slumped to the ground, motionless.

"Stupid man," hissed Domingo Dominguez. "No brains, no tact."

"Now then," mused the madman as he peered closely at Mack and Michael, "what were we talking about?"

Chapter 11: O'Boyles United

"Ain't no guarantees in hunting or in life, Son.
You know that. Now, c'mon...let's finish
what we started."

"I give you both credit for playing the game," said Domingo Dominguez, smiling as he spoke, "but the outcome was never really in any doubt, was it?"

Michael glanced at his father. They had foolishly underestimated Domingo's ability to track them. Both Michael and Mack had figured the explosive fire would have overcome their pursuers – at least temporarily – thereby giving them some breathing room, as well as much needed time to collect themselves and plan. Obviously, they had been very wrong.

"You two think you understand hunting and transgenics, but you really know nothing about either," boasted Domingo as he stepped forward. "Every tree, insect, blade of grass...I'm connected to it all. I have become king here!" Domingo was still dressed in his De Jaeger Enterprises hunting outfit. It appeared remarkably clean and undamaged. He carried no weapons other than his walking stick and seemed completely at ease as his viscous entourage wrapped around him in a state of perpetual malevolent motion.

"You're sick in the head, Dominguez," attested Mack. "We're on to you. We know what you're planning and we won't let you do it."

"Won't let me do it?" mocked Dominguez. "Who will stop me? You two are both walking dead men." As Dominguez said this, the entire circle of transgenics began to constrict against the father and son.

"Well, Dad," Michael apologized, "I'm real sorry I got you mixed-up in all this. I should have listened to you."

Mack paused for a second. He could feel the tears begin to well up in his eyes. He had just gotten his son back and now this crazy man was about to take everything away. No, he could not abide by that.

"Domingo, why are you doing this?" questioned Mack finally.

The short man did not bother to acknowledge the old hunter. His face was now highly animated, but his eyes looked dull and glazed over, almost dead. It was as if something else had taken over the lion's share of control. Dominguez was there, but outside forces seemed to be driving his thoughts.

"She has been gone for a long time, but now she has returned," spewed out Dominguez suddenly. "He sent the deluge of great waters forth and washed away her beautiful creation, but we have found a way to reestablish her kingdom. Her reemergence begins here." As Dominguez finished speaking, he gazed down at the agitated throngs of transgenic servants and smiled. The smug look on his face was greeted by a great uproar of horrible howls and wicked cackling.

Mack eyed the transgenics warily as he subtly slid his hand into his side pockets. "Not sure what his damage is," muttered the hunter to his son in a very low voice, "but this cat seems to have lost his mind. Like you said, the Domingo Dominguez I heard about was a drug-dealing scum bag who liked to go on expensive hunts, a high-functioning sociopath who liked to pull the trigger, but certainly not totally insane."

Michael said nothing as he lowered his gaze and prepared himself. He knew something big was about to happen.

"Wait until the beasties get to within a couple of feet and get ready to high tail it outta here," Mack whispered to Michael in a surprisingly assured tone.

"Everything on Earth has an Achilles' heel, Dominguez," shouted Mack defiantly as his eyes flashed at his pursuer, "even your transgenic super-soldiers." He then looked down at a quintuplet of vicious hyena-hybrid creatures. Their long muzzles were loaded with razor sharp teeth and their muscular haunches rippled beneath their taut spotted fur. They appeared frenzied and ready to spring at any moment.

"Listen up, you hideous freaks!" Mack screamed. "I've got something I want you to hear!" With that, Mack's hands shot outward. He was brazenly holding two plastic-covered, rounded rectangle shapes in front of the crazed animals. With a sudden, exaggerated squeezing motion from both of his weathered hands, the two plastic devices rapidly lit up in unison and emitted a shrill hyper-sonic screech which was barely perceptible to human ears.

Almost immediately, the encroaching transgenics lost all sense of cohesion and fell into complete disarray. Dominguez's confident smile suddenly gave way to a look of dismay as he watched the creatures bolt off pell-mell. During the ensuing tumult, he was physically repelled backwards as the hastily retreating horde charged back and forth, knocking each other down and trampling one another.

Taking advantage of the chaos, Mack grabbed his son by the arm. "C'mon," he urged Michael. "This is our last chance. These handheld hypersonics are just about out of juice. I found them on our way out of the lodge we torched. I was saving them for an emergency."

"Well, Dad," exclaimed Michael, "I'd say that qualified!"

As the two men ran, Mack once again glanced down to check the power level on the devices. Both were on their last bars and Mack could tell that the high-pitched wail was beginning to lessen in intensity. He estimated that the two of them would have ten minutes or less before the devices failed altogether. "It's time to pray to your Guardian Angel, Mick," said Mack, breathing hard as he ran. "We only have one more chance at this."

"Yeah," said Michael in response. "We're gonna need a miracle."

"Yep," agreed Mack, "that and some Semtex. How much more do you have?"

Michael reached back into his backpack as he continued to run through the heavy brush and in an instant, produced a seemingly non-descript brick of what was akin to gray Play-Doh. "I've got four field charges and three bricks of plastique," he managed to say between heavy breaths.

"You think that'll be enough?" Mack wondered as a very real sense of concern edged its way into his voice.

"Probably," replied Michael with only a hint of reservation. "We don't need to level the House or the generator. We just need to disrupt their inner workings."

Mack was feeling tired, bone tired, as he ran along. He was a very active guy, but the Preserve was proving itself to be a tough nut to crack. He was becoming more fatigued, thirsty, and hungry by the minute. Doubts about how much longer he could keep up this burdensome pace began to inch into his brain. His broken rib was still giving him major trouble and caused him searing pain every time he inspired. "We need...to split up, Michael," Mack managed to spit out between labored breaths. "As near as I can tell, the Birthing House is a couple of miles yonder," said Mack, pointing with a crooked finger in a northerly direction.

"No offense, Dad," advised Michael. "But you look like you're running out of steam. How are you going to get through the next three miles of transgenics? You'll die." Michael sounded genuinely distressed by his father's proposition he rush headlong into battle alone. It would be an impossible task for a fit, fresh young man, say nothing about the banged up old man. No, Michael did not like his dad's chances in the least.

"I appreciate the concern," said Mack, "I really do, but I've run the scenario in my head over and over. There is no other way. We have to shut this place down. You have the best chance of blowing the generator. It's at elevation and I'm already suckin' wind. I won't make it."

Michael looked pensively at his father. He understood his rationale, but he did not agree with it. "You know Dominguez has probably already hatched the total number of transgenics he needs," cautioned the young man. "There are power relays to the House, but the generator is still the biggest bang for our buck."

"I'm not disputing that, Michael," shot back Mack, "but I have a hunch and I need to let it play out. I think there is more going on here than meets the eye."

Michael said nothing more. He knew from past experience that when his father made up his mind about something, that was it. The old man was going to the Birthing House.

The two men suddenly trotted to a stop and just looked at each other for a brief moment. No words were exchanged, but Mack on the spur of the moment jutted his right hand out. Almost simultaneously, Michael did the same. Father and son grasped hands firmly and shook. "I'm proud of you, Boy," said Mack as his voice broke slightly. "I never could have asked for a better son."

Michael was now misty eyed as he stared at his father. He had aged a few years in the last several hours. He was very tired and his eyes were heavy. "Thanks, Dad," said Michael emotionally as he looked down at the ground and kicked a rock gently with his foot. "This might be it, then," he managed to say as he looked up at his father once more.

"Ain't no guarantees in hunting or in life, Son. You know that. Now, c'mon...let's finish what we started."

Michael said nothing. He handed his father half of the explosives and trigger devices in his backpack and veered off to the left. Just as he began running, his father called out, "Michael..."

The young O'Boyle stopped and turned to see his father's face looking right at him from across the open jungle.

"I love you," was all the older O'Boyle said. With that, Mack disappeared into the dense vegetation.

"I love you, too, Dad," whispered Michael as he once again turned and began running for the generator.

Chapter 12: Birthing House Surprises

Suddenly, the pachyderm-creature opened both
of its eyes and stared directly across the
glass tank enclosure at Mack.

As the minutes ticked by, Mack was forced to slow down substantially. A deep, aching fatigue had made its ugly presence known and he was reduced to rapid walking. His chest wall burned and he felt he had to increasingly work to get enough air as he plunged forward.

Just as he was convinced he could not take one more step, there, in the clearing before him, a solid concrete building constructed in the same style as the control center suddenly came into view. Mack could not help but think how truly repugnant looking the gray structure was. Ugly did not begin to describe the edifice and its strange contours.

A pride of transgenic lions mulled about along the front of the building. Their yellow bodies were spotted and several of the bigger males had hard crests projecting from behind their ears. In addition, a number of the lions possessed six legs, with the supernumerary appendages sporting unusually long, menacing claws.

Gonna need a distraction, ruminated Mack as he surveyed the formidable array of transgenic guards and then quickly glanced at his hypersonic emitter. It was dead. The single brightly lit bar had now been replaced by a somber black strip.

Mack crouched down low to the ground and began to move towards the east end of the building. He clutched the explosives tightly to his chest as he made his way through the dense foliage. As he came forward, he soon encountered the abandoned mag-rail train. It looked relatively untouched and in decent enough repair. A dull red light blinked on the main console, and the engine car continually emitted a low hum, as if to indicate it was at least minimally operational. While Mack inspected the structure, he noticed that the track line continued on to the back of the Birthing House. *The rail system somehow has power. Dominguez must have forgotten or doesn't care,* contemplated Mack. *I can use that to my advantage.*

Still maintaining a low crouch, Mack carefully made his way inside the lead mag-line car. The wind was in his face. With a wary eye on the animal sentries, he pressed a button labeled "forward" and the series of rail cars moaned to life and began steadily moving towards the large drab building.

The feline guardians' ears perked up immediately, and before Mack knew just what had happened, he was surrounded by the group of roaring adversaries. They careened aggressively towards his rail car, but as they neared to within several feet of the track, they suddenly pulled up and halted their attack. "Thank you, God!" Mack prayed with relief as he watched the looming cats pull away to within several feet of the tracks and proceed no further. "The trains' hypersonics are still partially operational."

The mag-rail continued to utter out a lonely hum as it slowly picked up speed and made its way forward. As it did, Mack watched closely out of both sides of the train car. He was literally surrounded by what appeared to be enemy forces. An unimaginable mishmash of transgenic animals had taken up positions along both sides of the carriage. Above him, he could see an assortment of weird birds and otherworldly looking winged mammals. They circled a safe distance away, never closing to more than a few dozen feet above the track line.

Mack's gamble had paid off. He was safe, for now. He knew that he was past the point of no return. If he couldn't find a way to access the Birthing House by way of the mag-line track, he was a sitting duck. He'd taken an immense risk, and, so far, he was moving towards his target. If the train lost power and he ended up marooned, it would only be a matter of time before he would be dead. Mack tried to not think about that glaring weak point in the plan, but his anxiety continued to rise as he made his way forward. His right hand moved up towards his chest to grasp his St. Hubertus medal tightly as the series of rail cars rolled onward.

As Mack ruminated and prayed over his next plan of action, he soon spied the sturdy side service door. It was closed and showed no signs of opening as his conveyance approached. This was not good. He needed to get inside and fast. He reminded himself that if he were stranded in the carriage, he was done and there was absolutely no hope of stopping Dominguez.

When the carriage pulled to within five feet of the imposing lowered access door, it suddenly shuddered to life and began to roll up. The army of transgenic animals continued to stay at bay, standing their ground and only watching in ominous silence as the door opened fully, exposing the dark interior of the Birthing House. Without missing a beat, the mag-rail train continued humming as it moved into the building. "Thank you, God!" yelped Mack in a prayer of thanksgiving once again as he traveled through the open door.

He was in! So far, things had gone really smoothly. He hated to look a gift horse in the mouth, but the skeptic in him felt that maybe he had experienced too easy a go of it so far. He tried to push these thoughts from his mind, but could not dismiss what his gut was telling him. He would have to be on guard.

Mack quickly opened his worn satchel and inspected the contents. His explosives were all accounted for. He now had to make his way to the guts of the machinery and blow this place sky-high. He prayed Michael was having an equal amount of success finding and disabling the generators. Mack understood the incredible responsibility he and his son shared given their wild and weird foray into the Mega-Preserve. Failure was not an option.

As the mag-line track terminated, Mack could feel the carriage come to a surprisingly smooth stop. Looking all around the dimly lit facility, he scanned for signs of danger. As he did, he could see the broad service doors begin to close behind him. *Was the coast clear? Had some of the transgenics from outside managed to slip inside the facility in spite of the hypersonic shielding?* Mack could not be sure, but he really had no choice but to take a chance and step outside of the carriage. Time was of the essence and he needed to keep moving forward.

As he cautiously made his way out onto the hard concrete floor, he listened intently for any signs of danger. The soft sound of humming machines was heard all around him, but his old eyes could not detect any overt signs of movement. Standing motionless, Mack looked to his left and then to his right. As he did, he carefully peered down several long hallways. His thoughts raced back to the control tower and his mind's eye tried to reproduce the Birthing House map he had quickly scanned before his hasty retreat. The architectural layout was similar to a wheel hub with many spokes. Mack estimated that he was on the extreme eastern side. He needed to make his way to the left, plant the explosives, and get clear.

Walking in what he believed was the correct direction, Mack found himself increasingly concerned by what he

166

saw. The interior of the building was reinforced concrete and metal; it quite literally had the look and feel of a bomb shelter. He needed to find the main birthing chamber. Once there, he could make a decision as to where to set his charges to get the most bang for his buck. He would have only one chance at this. If he fell short in damaging enough infrastructure, he would fail to shut down the facility completely.

The only sounds Mack could hear now were the soft tapping of his boots and the reverberating sound they made down the long hallway. As he cautiously passed along the wall, he noticed several side alcoves and fluid filled tanks. Some looked to be empty, while others held embryonic-like material in various stages of development. The developing organisms did not move and their pale, white skin was ghostly and devitalized. The entire scene gave off an eerie *Island of Dr. Moreau* vibe and he could feel his skin begin to crawl as he continued on.

As he walked farther, Mack began to notice more and more of the side alcoves. They gave the impression of being a maze within a maze. Various alien-looking organisms were suspended in the glass containment vessels and the size of the containers steadily increased. Glancing quickly inside, Mack took note of the rudimentary animal shapes floating within each. The more substantial and developed embryonic specimens were more easily distinguished. Immediately, he recognized feline, canine, and avian species intermixed among the various tanks.

After taking a moment to process the remarkable diversity of animal shapes, Mack noticed a dim light up ahead. Continuing on, he soon found himself in a cavernous, open room. Like the hallway he had just traversed, this place was filled with similarly styled clear, cylindrical containers.

They differed from those he had seen alongside the hallway in that these elegant looking cylinders were massive, several orders of magnitude bigger than anything he had witnessed in the smaller side alcove tanks. Measuring in at nearly forty feet wide and twelve feet tall, Mack felt his breath leave his body as he stared at the array of transgenic organisms now before him. It was a collection of animals the likes of which he had never dreamed of.

Placing his hand on the smooth, glass-like container closest to him, Mack peered long and hard at the creature inside. It was a strange hippo-like animal with a hostile set of yellowish-white tusks and deep black fur. Its sturdy face gently swayed back and forth within the clear liquid exhibiting an almost rhythmic motion. Mack moved his face closer to the glass as he continued to peer in on the beast. He was captivated by the amazing detail and symmetry of the animal's form. It was, in all honesty, horrible and beautiful to behold at the same time.

Suddenly, the pachyderm-creature opened both of its eyes and stared directly across the glass tank enclosure at Mack. Evidently it had found its peace disturbed and the monstrous organism's body actively spasmed to life, kicking its limbs in unison. Mack stepped back several steps, surprised and scared by the unexpected turn of events. As he did, he noticed that the entire room of liquid-immersed transgenic creatures abruptly came alive, opened their eyes, and stared intently at him.

"Enough dilly-dallying," he muttered, reprimanding himself. "I've got a job to do!" Mack unexpectedly found himself conflicted regarding the planned destruction of this facility. As he observed all of the exquisitely complex animals before him, he wondered if there just might be another way to combat the danger this place represented without having to kill everything inside it.

Mack racked his brain for a potential solution. He had made it to the heart of what he believed to be the major transgenic production facility. This was his chance to strike a decisive blow against Domingo's perverted plan to wreck the world. *Why was he having second thoughts? He needed to stick with the plan, right? What other option did he have?*

He rifled through his satchel to retrieve the explosives, but an ominous pair of yellow eyes piercingly engaged Mack from across the room. The glowing amber orbs gradually began to get bigger and bigger as Mack listened to the steady approach of heavy footsteps.

"Oh no," groaned Mack as he quickly looked up at the towering figure and hastily began to shuffle back. He must be getting daft in his old age. He should have known this place would have some manner of transgenic watchdogs. To imagine otherwise was just plain stupid. Things had been going way too smoothly thus far. Mack kicked himself for letting his guard down and being so eager.

As he pulled back farther towards the wall, he was immediately struck by how tall the incoming shadowy mass was. The facility had high, vaulted-ceilings that he guesstimated to be at least ten feet in height and this thing looked like it almost scraped them with its head. The hulking mass was bipedal, not four-legged like the rest of the transgenics he had encountered. In spite of its massiveness, the thing moved with a coordination and symmetry that worried Mack. *Gotta move*, he decided.

Taking several more steps back, Mack's right hand squeezed the plastic explosive. Reaching deeper into his bag, he quickly found his detonators and held them out in front on himself. "I've got something for you, buddy!" yelled Mack across the room. "One step closer and I blow this place sky-high."

There was no response. Either his attacker didn't understand his threat or it didn't care. With no warning, a long vine-like hand suddenly careened forward and snatched the bomb material away from him. In another instant, Mack felt the same rough hand push him tightly against the wall with a level of preternatural strength he had only felt demonstrated by the most powerful of wild animals. He was immediately pinned up against the cold concrete edifice and could not move a muscle.

Peering up at his assailant from against the wall, Mack watched as the alarming yellow orbs came more closely into view. As the massive figure made its way into the dim light, Mack let out a gasp. He could feel his heart rate accelerate and his breathing quicken. In all his years of hunting transgenics, he had never encountered anything like this. *Was it a man or an animal?* He couldn't be sure. "What are you?" he managed to spit out.

The menacing figure did not say anything. It continued to stare straight ahead with unblinking, impassive eyes as it pressed forward with its prodigious strength.

The being before him was truly terrifying. It was well over nine feet tall, covered in coarse dark hair, and adorned with an assortment of feather-like shapes on its shoulders. The man-thing possessed a rotund barrel-shaped chest and its shoulders rippled with muscles. Its legs were long and each lower appendage was attached to a jet-black cloven hoof. Mack could just make out a long hairless tail swaying back and forth behind the ugly being. It noiselessly flittered in a whip-like motion and reminded Mack of a big cat.

Without a single utterance, another long arm jumped out at Mack. The wieldy appendage flashed forward to secure its captive's free left arm.

Though space was limited, Mack was able to shimmy his body off to the right, feeling the rush of air as the wooly arm just missed him by inches. Whether the towering creature was trying to incapacitate, restrain, or kill him, Mack did not know. Regardless of his opponent's ultimate motivation, Mack desperately needed to get away. Suddenly remembering that he still had Tanaka's tanto, he reached into his belt, produced the razor sharp blade, and brought it to bear mere inches from his assailant. As the creature lunged forward once again, his efforts were met with a quick pushing movement from Mack's sole free arm. The Japanese blade buried itself deep into the hairy torso of his wild attacker and a rush of hot blood emerged from the hastily created wound.

A horrible, inhumane wail emerged from the wounded creature and it echoed throughout the concrete chamber. Tanaka's knife had struck deep inside the thing's side and Mack decided that it must have lodged between ribs given his inability to retrieve the sharp blade. The two-legged animal-thing twisted away from him rapidly, thus the tanto was completely forced from his hand. Mack was now weaponless and he stared at the monstrous form as its loud bellows continued.

Menacingly, the scary yellow eyes stared down at Mack. In an instant, they began to narrow into fiery, elongated slits.

171

With a second series of horrifying howls, the fearsome thing drew itself up to his full height, prompting Mack to think that the fuming beast was going to attack him yet another time. He had stabbed the mammoth creature in the chest. It obviously did not like getting tagged with the tanto, but it had not really slowed him down much. Mack searched the room for some other weapon.

While he groped around for something with which to fight back, the creature forged ahead towards his opponent. In an instant, Mack felt the inhumanely strong set of hands grip him by the shoulder and neck, simultaneously hoisting him off the floor and squeezing him viscously. He screamed out in pain as his assailant arms tightened and compressed his body in unnatural ways. It was impossible to breathe and he could feel his muscles quiver and fail under the unrelenting strain from the creature's vice-like grip.

Black spots began to appear along the periphery of his visual fields and Mack's brain felt muddled as much due to the pain as the lack of oxygen. He had been pulled to within several inches of the gruesome beast's face. A renewed sense of dread overcame him as he stared into the monster's twisted visage. For several long seconds, the irate assailant simply stared at Mack with its glowing amber eyes. The hunter felt his adversary's hot breath assail his forehead and he logically expected the coup de grace to be delivered at any moment, but the finishing blow never came. As the creature studied him, an odd sense of familiarity quietly began to assert itself between the monster and his now helpless opponent.

The face before him possessed a harsh, alien shape with unnatural, elongated features. The creature's mouth was agape slightly, and Mack noticed the alarming series of

172

sharp teeth and almost tusk-like canines. In spite of all of this, Mack knew that this was Bram de Jaeger. The underlying resemblance was unmistakable.

"B-Bram?" Mack managed to blurt out as the creature continued to manhandle him.

"Stop!" called out a voice from across the darkened room.

Mack felt an immediate loosening of the death grip and he slid to the floor in a crumpled heap. Looking up at his attacker, Mack watched as the loathsome animal-thing stepped back dutifully and simply stood there, continually staring at Mack with those same unblinking deep amber eyes. It did not make a sound.

Mack turned to meet his intercessor. His lungs were still recovering from the intense crushing he had experienced and the prior broken rib continued to ache with each inhalation. His brain was muddled from the lack of oxygen and he struggled to take in several deep breaths to compensate. "W-what's goin' on around here?" he finally managed to say.

"Bram" remained completely silent. His only response to Mack's question was to step aside and fade back into the shadows from which he had emerged only a few moments ago. As he did so, Mack could see that a much smaller, female figure was standing directly behind his attacker. When the petite woman stepped closer and bent down next to Mack, a feeling of astonishment mixed with relief overtook him and he could not help but smile. It was none other than Dr. Josephine Fox.

The young woman smiled as her eyes met Mack's, seemingly genuinely pleased to see the old hunter.

"Fox!" stammered Mack. "I figured you were dead!"

Josephine Fox nodded her head sadly, acknowledging the unprecedented danger she'd recently been plunged into. Her eyes were glassy and her lower lip quivered slightly as she slowly spoke. "It's a long story, Mr. O'Boyle," replied Fox with her same eerily familiar voice. "Suffice to say, many things have happened since we last saw one another."

Chapter 13: A Cave and Its Contents

"You have caught a glimpse of the future,
Dr. O'Boyle. What do you think?"

Michael O'Boyle had been hunting his entire life. Tracking, stalking, and taking game was in his blood and he loved it. Cape buffalo, elephant, or lion - it didn't matter. He had hunted them all and he never really worried about his safety or questioned what he was doing.

But now, as he looked around at the wild, alien jungle environment he found himself thrust into, he could think of nothing else. He was scared, probably more scared than he had ever been in his life. As he made his way towards the emergency generator, he could not help but dwell on what was at stake and the consequences of failure.

Thus far, he had done a fairly good job of avoiding Dominguez's army. He had not encountered the larger organisms and the multitude of smaller, quicker transgenics had not yet located him. He estimated that he was only a mile or so from the emergency generator location. Once he arrived, Michael planned to recon the area, set his charges, and then clear out. He tried not to think about what might happen if he became trapped and could not escape outside the blast radius. The moment this job turned into a suicide mission, he would have to do some really quick assessments and make some hard choices. For now, he simply prayed that he could avoid that particular scenario altogether.

As he hurried along, Michael noticed that the terrain was beginning to become more alpine in appearance. The grassy jungle floor was gradually giving way to rocks and low scrub. The air temperature lowered and Michael shivered slightly as he braced himself against a harsh, blowing wind.

The Mega-Preserve truly was a wonder to behold: multiple biomes were fully contained and integrated inside a single facility. No other company could boast of such a unique set-up. Michael had been, and still was, in awe of the place. The 32 diverse sectors and the totally unique transgenics in them were quite an achievement. That being said, he really wished his booney tights were still working. They went off-line soon after the Preserve had been turned upside down. Their thermo-regulator functions had gone caput, and the torn underclothes now provided only minimal protection against the elements.

As he braced himself against the cold, Michael noticed some discarded rebar, metal conduit, and other pieces of scrap metal on the rocky surface. All around him were the abandoned remnants of electrical and communications equipment used in the creation of the back-up generator several hundred meters away. One piece of conduit in particular held a nice sharp, beveled edge and was surprisingly light to the touch. As he hoisted it up, Michael was reminded of his father's friend, Alistair. He had always maintained an impressive collection of African weapons, primarily spears and clubs. This found piece of metal was nearly the exact shape and weight of a Maasai spear. With a few minor alterations and a bit of elbow grease, Michael was convinced he could make it function like just like the deadly weapon it resembled.

Shifting the long metal object between his worn hands, a slight smile emerged on his weather-beaten face. It really was amazing what you could scavenge if you had the imagination. Besides, he was down to his last two arrows. The time it took to find materials, flint nap arrow heads, and fletch the tails adequately was not something he had in abundance right now. This improvised spear would have to do. If he could fashion an atlatl at some point in the future, then all the better.

Michael's musings were disrupted by surging figures that had emerged from the scrub pines and brush several hundred yards away. A trio of intense-looking, canine-like transgenics was making its way towards him in a dead sprint. Michael watched with alarm as they burst over the rocky terrain, moving as sure as mountain goats. They bounded over the low lying vegetation and boulders as if the obstacles were not even there. *Wild dogs*, Michael urgently said to himself. *Pack hunters. Gotta find cover fast!*

With that, Michael turned to flee. As he did, he briefly looked over his shoulder to see his pursuers. They were rapidly gaining on him. At this rate, they would be on him in no time. He had no hope of outrunning the pack and he knew he needed to hide. He had to think of something quick.

A cursory scan of the immediate area revealed groupings of tall pines dotting the mountainside before him and a chain of ravines and crevasses which peppered the rocky outcroppings just above them. Michael more closely studied the area directly ahead of him and noticed a small chasm just to the right of the nearest ravine. Deciding that he had nothing to lose, Michael sprinted forward and within seconds found himself entering the mouth of a moderate sized cave. As he slid along the shale covered surface, he could feel the jagged rocks dig into his already torn clothes and bruised skin.

The external ambient light began to fade quickly as the young hunter plunged deeper into the labyrinthine gloom. As pitched darkness encroached further, Michael paused for a moment and looked back towards his pursuers. Suddenly, without warning, a boorish black shape made its way furiously towards his head. Grasping his makeshift spear with both hands, he thrust it out with all his might. In an instant, he felt a forceful impact and was tossed backward against the cave wall. The blunt end of his metal spear had forcibly lodged into the stony cave floor. There, buried to the mid-shaft, was the once defiant transgenic canine. The beastly terror squirmed and bared its teeth as its life force ebbed. After a few more seconds of futile struggling, the creature expired and a dark pool of blood formed on the cave floor beneath him. The metal conduit from which the hasty spear had been fashioned was bent at a forty-five degree angle. The mighty transgenic beast hung on the twisted cable like a massive piece of meat on an overburdened skewer.

Relieved to be alive, but convinced he was still not in the clear, Michael turned and ran as expeditiously as he could into the depths of the cave, plunging farther and farther into the blackness. Michael could still hear the yelping, angry calls from his dead antagonist's fellow pursuers reverberate throughout the cave. He had a small survival flashlight in his possession and he hurriedly turned it on.

As he progressed into the cave, he soon found himself in increasingly tight confines. He was now forced to crouch down and angle his body in order to continue.

The major advantage that the narrowing cave walls held was that they were certainly too tight for his pursuers to pass through. Still, Michael worried about going too far into the cavern. If he was not careful, he might become trapped and then he would be no good to anybody. Worse yet, he could become lost and never make it out. *How long would the flashlight last? Two hours with continuous use? That might not be enough time.* The other option was to turn and make a stand. He had lost his spear as quickly as he had found it and the bow was no good to him in such confined spaces. He still had a bush machete, but that would not be enough against the viscous transgenic dogs. No, the only option was to continue on, at least for the time being.

Just as Michael was beginning to think he could not proceed any farther, the rocky enclosure gradually began to expand. After several more steps, he was startled to see what could only be some sort of artificial light. It pulsed many meters up ahead and the glow it gave off was like nothing Michael had ever encountered.

Within seconds, the young hunter found himself peering into a gigantic rocky chamber. Steam and hot gasses boiled all around him. Glowing molten material streamed out into the subterranean cavern, forming hundreds of meandering red hot veins. The emblazoned material ran across the floor of the immeasurable stone amphitheater in crimson rivulets forming a spider-web maze of glowing lines. *Geo-thermals everywhere*, meditated Michael. It seemed as though the capacious cathedral-like structure went on forever.

As Michael continued to scan the gigantic room, his attention rapidly shifted to the very center of the grand, hollowed out space. There, situated equidistantly from each of the arching stone walls, was a series of white, upright columns and cylindrical structures. At first, Michael thought they might be some sort of odd stalagmite formations, but upon closer inspection, Michael could see that they were nothing of the sort. As he strained his eyes, he could just make out a pulsing rhythm coursing through organic spires and elliptical shapes. Michael estimated that the entire framework had to measure at least 100 meters across. It was tall, too, at least 20 meters in height. With careful observation, he noted that the sky-high system swayed slightly and the semi-transparent "skin" made a show of almost breathing as it tensed and released every few seconds.

What was that thing? There was certainly no record of it in the initial designs of the Mega-Preserve. *Who had built it? What was its purpose? Why was it situated here?*

Then before him, one of the cylindrical hanging pods began to shudder and shake. As if on cue, the long, arching arm of its suspending spire dutifully began to dip and lower. Soon the elliptical hanging structure adeptly peeled back and disgorged its previously obscured contents.

Michael watched in stunned silence at what happened next: a quivering bag of dark material had been released from the massive container. After several seconds, a run of spastic arching motions commenced beneath the taut material. Then, without warning, a trembling, clawed extremity emerged, promptly followed by a small set of snapping jaws. Within mere moments, the slimy bag had been discarded altogether and there, standing next to the pulsing white structure, was what could only be described as a newborn transgenic.

As the unmistakably dog-like creature stood upon its shaking legs, Michael continued observing with a mix of horror and extreme curiosity as the canid slowly began to find its footing. The beast staggered over to the base of the towering white spire that had served as it suspended home only moments ago. There, it extended its face forward in an unmistakable rooting motion. No sooner had it done this than the white spire began to splice itself open and then partially envelope the swaying creature standing before it. The canid-like transgenic's head and front quarters disappeared, but the remainder of its thin body stood outside the organic structure. As it did, the once swaying creature grew steadier on its legs. Within seconds, the transgenic began to increase in size dramatically, nearly doubling its birth weight. It was now approximately half the size of the canine-creature Michael had killed just inside the cave entrance. The beast was partially covered with coarse, dark hair, and its feet and claws had grown prodigiously. Although not as formidable as the other full-grown creations he had witnessed inside the Mega-Preserve, it was obvious that this beast had the potential to become another of Dominguez's unholy engines of death and destruction. *Was this animal to serve as the dead dog-beast's replacement?*

Forget the Birthing House or the emergency generators, concluded Michael, *Gamekeeper has bypassed all of that. This is a genuine freak factory or I'm the King of Siam. I'm going to have to blow this place to smithereens.*

Michael surveyed the massive chamber, deep in thought. *How much plastique would it take to implode this chamber? Would it disable the transgenic monster maker? Would it kill most of the fetal transgenics?* Michael couldn't be sure, but his gut told him that this bizarre place held the key to stopping Dominguez's insane plan. *Did he have all the answers? Most definitely not.* In spite of that, his instincts told him this otherworldly production facility was beyond evil and, given all that had happened inside the Preserve, no quarter would be given. The Law of the Jungle had subsumed all else in this place and Michael recognized immediately what he must do.

After several more seconds of scanning the area and the unfolding macabre scene far beneath him, Michael guesstimated that the whole "room" was at least a half mile in diameter. If he placed charges at 12, 3, 6, and 9 o'clock, he figured he would have a good chance of blowing the whole cave network up. He hoped he had enough detonation cord and charges to cover the area, but soon stopped performing calculations in his head. His dad used to say, "Go big or go home," and that was exactly what the current situation called for.

Michael began to inspect the craggy walls behind him. Small streams of liquid water had formed on the rocks and made a dripping sound next to him. As he walked farther, he came to a natural stone pillar that seemed to jut upwards in a tangle of limestone. It glistened along its surface as more water droplets formed along its length.

Neither Josephine nor Bram had ever told him about any large subterranean network inside the Mega-Preserve. The idea that something this large could be inside the facility and there was no documentation on any map or engineering schematic sent a chill down his spine. *Somebody knew about this place. Was this what Tanaka was really looking for?* He would get his answers, but this unnatural place needed to be dealt with first.

I blow a couple of these rock columns and I'm hoping the whole place implodes, discerned Michael as he again surveyed his petrous surroundings. *This rock is soft and full of moisture.*

Satisfied that he at least had a workable plan, Michael busied himself with his self-appointed task. Over the next 15 minutes, he successfully deposited his deadly cargo in a cruciform pattern. With this done, he consolidated his triggering devices and stopped to plan his next action.

Peering down across the vast lava strewn floor, Michael took in the full view of the globose white structure. He quickly noticed that the "Mother Monster" had become more active. What had begun as simply random movements in the long spire-like arms was now a course of frenetic motions. The birthing scenario Michael had witnessed earlier was beginning again in earnest. *It's making more replacement killers,* deduced Michael. *Best get out of here ASAP.*

As the young hunter made it back to his original cavernous entry point, he thought about his father. *Had he been successful in his mission? Had he been captured? Had he been...?* Michael did not want to think about it. He had just reconciled with the old man and he might never see him again. Doubts began to creep into his mind. *What if his plan failed and Domingo could still export his transgenic agricultural terrorism and only God knew what else to the outside world? What was the connection between the thing inside the cave, Gamekeeper, the Birthing Houses, and the murderous Domingo? Was this thing the 'Her' he had referred to earlier?*

No, answered Michael to himself. *Focus on the task at hand!* This was his best shot. Every moment out in the open inside the Preserve was a chance of being discovered and killed. Finding this place was a gift. It had all the trappings of a den. Instinctively, he knew he was in the belly of the beast. If he didn't take advantage of it now, he was a fool.

Michael took stock of his trigger devices one more time. His remote detonators should have a strong enough signal to reach all of the charges as long as he was not too far inside the entrance cave when he detonated them. At this point, he saw no signs of any transgenics. His attackers from earlier seemed to have abandoned the area once he had disappeared through the tight, rocky passage.

With this in mind, Michael stepped back into the cave opening from which he had originally descended. He clung to the devices tightly as he squeezed back into the rough, narrow space. As he neared the site where he had killed the canine transgenic, he was shocked to see that the carcass was gone. All that was left was his bent, metal spear and a pool of partially congealed blood. Michael bent down to inspect the scene with his small flashlight in hand. This was bizarre. *Where was the body?* The dead transgenic dog was not small by any stretch of the imagination. In fact, Michael estimated that the thing was well over 200 pounds. *What could have removed a creature like that?*

"You have caught a glimpse of the future, Dr. O'Boyle. What do you think?" Michael quickly looked up startled by the revelation that something else was nearby. Without delay, he noticed there, standing just before him, was Domingo Dominguez. He was flanked on all sides by the very same canid transgenics that had pursued Michael into the cave initially. They each let out low, guttural growls, but did not twitch a muscle. Their crazed eyes focused like lasers on the hunter, and they stood statue still.

"I think you're sick and extremely dangerous," said Michael as he warily stood to his feet, all the while staring back at the aggressive horde and their malevolent master. He had dreaded being in this position, but the madman before him forced his hand. It was now or never. If he did not detonate the charges immediately, he may not get another opportunity.

"I don't know what the connection is between you and that monster in the cave, but I know it can't be good. I'm gonna blow you and this disgusting freak show to bits." With that, Michael reached down and defiantly slammed the plungers on his triggering devices with a resounding thud. He stood there bravely with a steady look of determination on his grim face, but nothing happened. No explosion, no sound, no rush of air. *Nothing*.

"Oh, Dr. O'Boyle," said Dominguez with a patronizing tone. "Did you really think I would let you destroy such a wonderful achievement? You have been given a front row seat to the dawn of a new era, yet you simply want to react with fear, like some diminutive forest creature. I thought a man of science would be more open-minded to progress. After all, we are only setting things back the way they used to be...the way they should be."

As his seemingly demented pursuer finished speaking, it summarily occurred to Michael that Domingo Dominguez had changed. The man's speech patterns, mannerisms, and even his height seemed altered. The Dominguez he had met two days ago spoke with a slight Spanish accent and was no more than 5 feet 5 inches tall and overweight. The man confronting him now was at least 6 feet tall and had the features of someone far more robust and athletic.

Looking into his dark eyes, Michael took note of how dull they appeared. If the eyes were the mirror to the soul, Dominguez's reflective surfaces were thoroughly cracked, if not completely blackened. Something very strange was happening and a steady horror began to creep into Michael brain as he entertained the possible explanations for the abnormal metamorphosis. It certainly seemed that the man's very essence, in addition to his physical appearance, was being rapidly renovated in a most peculiar way. What had seemed to be the make-believe, deluded ravings of a madman only hours earlier now displayed a weirdly evil plausibility that sent a shudder through Michael.

A series of clicking and snapping noises suddenly echoed through the cave system. In an instant, a stream of Dominguez's black beetle servants erupted from the recesses behind Michael. The army of insects carried the wrecked remains of the explosives Michael had installed only a few short moments ago. The plastic components were jostled about as if they were floating on a wavy midnight black sea.

Michael felt an immediate sense of repulsion and reflexively stepped back as the parade of beetles and disassembled explosives made its way around his feet. From primates to arthropods, the unfolding scene suggested that Domingo controlled them all with equal ease. Michael shook his head with disgust as well as a begrudging sense of respect for the psychopath and his murderous minions. The science behind them – if that was what it could even be called – escaped him completely. He had been outclassed and it made him outraged.

"It's not over, yet," shot back Michael angrily. "My father is still out there."

"Yes," replied Domingo bluntly. "He is. The final hunt is about to begin."

"You got that right, weirdo," muttered Michael as he planted his right foot behind him and lunged forward at Dominguez. If this was his last stand, he was going to go down swinging. It was a long shot, but he had nothing to lose. When Michael was within inches of Dominguez, a mess of snapping jaws and powerful, clawed paws swiftly intercepted him, forcing him up, backwards, and down to the hard, rocky ground. Craning his head up, Michael could just faintly see the shape of a large hunting boot rushing towards his face. Then, in an instant, everything went black.

Chapter 14: Gamekeeper 2.0

"Those things look...demonic,"
continued Mack, not waiting for a reply,
"straight up from the pits of hell."

Mack made a concerned motion towards the yellow-eyed monster now standing only a few feet from his present position. "What about him?" he said, gesturing towards the giant, now shadow cloaked figure.

"Bram won't hurt you," Dr. Fox said reassuringly. "He got here before I could and it looks like he may have been a little combative in his approach. He has been..."

Dr. Fox stopped speaking for a moment as her tired eyes peered over at the silent living monolith. She seemed uncharacteristically lost for words, however she continued, "He's been altered and doesn't talk much, but I think he understands what is happening."

"Altered?" muttered Mack incredulously. "I guess you could say that."

"Please come with me," said Fox. "We have much more to discuss."

As Mack followed Dr. Fox, he found himself staring once again at the silent giant. It eyed the hunter ominously as it pawed at the embedded knife with a huge, hairy right hand.

While he walked away from the main birthing chamber and into what appeared to be a sweeping storage facility, he was greeted by a series of utterly bizarre sights. There stood Josephine Fox. All around her was an army of roving transgenics of various shapes and sizes: pachyderms, carnivores, and every type of animal amalgamation you could imagine.

"Josephine," Mack cautiously asked, "what is going on around here?"

"The Preserve," the scientist shot back. "We thought we could control the technology, but we were wrong...I was wrong." The petite scientist turned away slightly as tears began to gather along the corners of her bloodshot eyes. She gave "Bram" a quick sideways glance and buried her head in her hands. Mack stepped forward and placed his hand on the distraught woman's shoulder.

"Take it easy," he said as he attempted to console the crying woman. "Take your time and don't leave anything out. You can start by explaining what in the world happened to De Jaeger."

"Well," said Fox finally as she struggled to calmly compose herself, "when it was attacked, I believe Gamekeeper decided it needed to purge its systems. The original programming was being overridden and the defense protocols were enacted. It may not seem like it now, but I had written in some meaningful safeguards to protect the people and animals inside the Preserve. The Gamekeeper program recognized that it was being pushed out of the way and its primary directive is, and continues to be, regulation of the Mega-Preserve environment. The only way for it to reassert control was by getting off the sidelines and putting itself directly into the hunting environment."

"So it made De Jaeger into a transgenic zombie freak?" alleged Mack with an incredulous voice. "Where is that in its programming? Did you honestly cook that up as a contingency plan?"

"Bram was nearly dead when he was taken to the Birthing House," explained Fox as she cleared her throat and wiped her partially tear-streaked face. "Gamekeeper kept him alive by dispatching a sub-cadre of dogbats to intervene and take him away from the control tower. It was the only way to save his life after he had been mortally wounded during the initial attack. When he arrived here, Bram had lost a great deal of blood and was essentially brain dead. Gamekeeper used his failing brain to store what was left of the original programming before it was completely co-opted."

"Whoa," said Mack, "you are telling me that this hairy beast was not only once Bram de Jaeger, but that he is now all that is left of your Gamekeeper program?"

"Yes," replied Fox, "I'm afraid that is correct. I believe that a pirate program corrupted Gamekeeper's operating system to such a degree that the only viable option the computer could come up with was to store itself on a new hard drive, an organic network, if you will. This was not really much of a stretch given the fact that Gamekeeper's primary function is the design, assemblage, and direction of specific transgenic animal species."

Mack was not sure how to respond. He had seen and done some extraordinary things the last several days, but the weirdness factor just took a momentous leap forward. Creating transgenic animals for an accelerated Evo-Hunt was fantastic enough, but to have the capability to transfer computer code into the brain of a dead CEO? That seemed to be a stretch that even his open mind was having trouble dealing with. "So Gamekeeper has been more or less replaced by this pirate program?" queried Mack. "That is what is running the Preserve right now?"

"Yes," answered Fox. "The program's name is Matron."

"And all these transgenics," asked Mack, "why aren't they attacking?"

"Gamekeeper still maintains some semblance of control over a very small section of the species in the Preserve. These were all the game species created in advance of Matron's introduction and subsequent complete take over. It's a minority, but it is something," explained Fox.

"I have to tell you, Josephine," said Mack resolutely, "I thought you were dead for sure."

Dr. Fox nodded in agreement, all too aware of her given frailties and knew better than most what a viciously deadly place the Preserve had been transformed into. "Tanaka and I were attacked once we had crossed the river. He was mauled badly, but we still managed to make it to one of the hunting chalets. He told me he was sent here by a group of people because they suspected that someone inside the Preserve was planning to use my technology as a bio-weapon. He explained that there is more to what is happening than meets the eye and that the human actors are just chess pieces being moved about on a much larger board. I asked him to expound further what he meant by that, but Dominguez attacked us again and killed Tanaka. He would have killed me as well, but Gamekeeper showed up and brought me here."

Fox motioned to the emotionless man-thing standing over her. It said nothing and continued to look on with an impassive stare. "With Gamekeeper's help, I've been able to piece together what has happened inside the Mega-Preserve and what is happening to us."

Mack shook his head not sure he had heard Fox correctly. "You said, 'happening to us'. What do you mean by that?"

"With the introduction of the Matron program, the Mega-Preserve environment has become highly mutagenic," explained Fox. "Everything inside it is either brought in line with the ecosystem or destroyed. We have survived for over 24 hours. While we have been here, we have been bitten by insects, exposed to novel fungi, viral, and bacteria species, as well as transgenic blood products and saliva. Each of our individual physiologies is effectively altered."

"Altered?" challenged Mack. "I don't feel any different."

"No," replied Fox. "You won't. The changes will be subtle at first, but every moment we stay inside this place will make it harder to leave. I am hypothesizing that our skin and gut flora have already been considerably replaced. We've inhaled particulate matter and been exposed to so many novel antigens that I fear our bodies may never be able to tolerate reintroduction to the outside world."

"How can you be so sure?" said Mack skeptically. "Do you have any real proof?"

Dr. Fox reached into her pocket and produced a small date-like fruit. She proceeded to peel it and held it up for the Mack to inspect. "You remember the last time I ate this variety of fruit?" she recalled. "It made me ill almost immediately. Now, watch what happens." Without another word, Josephine Fox placed the peeled fruit in her mouth and began to chew. After several seconds, she swallowed and simply stood there.

Mack watched the scientist closely for several tense moments. After a minute had passed, she looked over at him and gave him a wry smile.

"No adverse affects," she mused. "However, I did open an MRE several hours ago and the very smell of the food inside made me sick to my stomach. I tasted the contents and gagged."

"So this new program just wants to rewrite our DNA and turn us into what? Creatures like Bram?" challenged Mack, shaking his head.

"The Matron program is in complete control and it has a very specific agenda," responded Fox. "We hoped we could incapacitate it by shutting down power or overhauling the Birthing House, but the program doesn't require any of the Mega-Preserve's conventional equipment to make new transgenic specimens."

"What are you saying?" argued Mack. "This Matron thing is making transgenics from scratch? No test tubes, computers, or birthing chambers? Now that IS impossible!"

"I didn't want to believe it either," said Dr. Fox, "but it's true. Gamekeeper showed me. Dominguez's operation is now independent of any of the Mega-Preserve's existing infrastructure. He's created a massive, semi-autonomous organic installation with pretty much unlimited production capabilities."

Mack stood in stunned silence in the midst of the transgenics. When he had first learned of the Preserve's unprecedented capacity to produce organisms, the mere idea seemed entirely impossible. It was only after he had witnessed the transgenics in the Mega-Preserve itself that he was fully able to wrap his head around what was happening. Now, he was being presented with another paradigm shift.

"If what you are saying is correct," finally replied Mack, "then we have to find this place and shut it down."

"Yes," answered Fox. "Our first goal must be containment."

"Any idea where this autonomous Birthing House is situated?" asked Mack. "I mean, if this thing is operating off the existing grid, where is it getting the power to do what it's doing?"

"C-caves," slowly spoke a voice from across the large room. "I-in caves."

Both Mack and Fox gazed at the giant figure standing behind them. Its coarse tusk-filled jaw had managed to speak those few words; however, just as quickly, the hulking beast turned silent once more.

"Geothermals," Fox explained to Mack. "Gamekeeper has some shared knowledge based on his interaction with the Matron program. He says there is a series of caves beneath the elevated plateau. Inside this place, there is a network of geothermal hotspots. That is what the Matron program is using to fuel its army."

"What about my son?" Mack worried. "What about Michael?"

Fox studied Gamekeeper's face. It just stared with impassive yellow-tinted eyes from the shadows. "He doesn't know," was all Fox said.

What do you mean, he doesn't know? Mack thought indignantly. The rules inside this insane place were constantly changing. What was supposed to be a fancy transgenic hunt had morphed into a death-defying rescue operation. Now, it all had the earmarks of the strange, world-threatening machinations of a madman, a rogue computer program, and a complete transformation of the planet as they all knew it.

"I'd really like to know just why Dominguez is doing this and what his connection to this Matron thing you mentioned is," growled Mack with a frustrated voice. "I mean, who's really running the show around here?"

"It's a bit nuanced," said Fox in response, "Gamekeeper understands Matron's programming to be more focused on world hegemony than world genocide. It doesn't want to kill the planet; it wants to control it. Once this new bio-technology is released out into the world, Gamekeeper's projections are that it would take only a matter of months for the entire planet to be reformed, probably irrevocably. As for Dominguez's role in all of this, Gamekeeper believes that he is only a tool in service to Matron."

"Only a tool, huh?" expressed Mack with incredulity.

"Yes," said Dr. Fox, "Dominguez is a criminal, but there is nothing in his dossier to suggest that he has any affiliation with any terrorist organizations. His criminal connections are limited to the narcotics trade and a semi-legitimate pharmaceutical and biotech company known as The Lightbringer Foundation."

"Lightbringer?" asked Mack quizzically. "Never heard of it. Some kind of think tank operating outside the law?"

"Gamekeeper could not tell me specifics and we have no access to the internet," replied Fox with a matter-of-fact tone in her voice. "I have heard of the Foundation only in passing, but I could not tell you much more than that."

After having said that, Josephine Fox stared down with an oddly pensive look on her face. Mack noticed it briefly, but quickly dismissed it as part of the woman's continued stress reaction.

"What did you mean when you said 'the planet would be reformed'?" questioned Mack after he gathered his train of thought. "Just like the fruit example?"

"Yes," said Fox, quickly looking up, "but that's only the beginning. These initial changes could, and most likely will, soon be followed by other more dramatic changes. We're talking about significant effects on the world populace - things like IQ, basic instinctual behavior, and even reproductive patterns."

"A bunch of dumbed-down slaves," interjected Mack. "Whoever is ultimately behind this wants to change the entire world into his or her own private Mega-Preserve." Mack mulled over the stunning implications of this plot. Rather than kill the world outright or hold it hostage, these maniacs would simply reform it in their own sick version of how they wished the world to be. From the sound of things so far, they would be the self-appointed master of all. To Mack's way of thinking, death would be a better option than being reduced to the level of an automaton slave.

"Dominguez and this Matron have to be stopped," offered Dr. Fox. "I just don't know how. They are in control of everything."

Mack absorbed the scientist's words for a moment. "Yeah," he replied, "you are 100 percent right about that."

Mack paused, deep in thought, as he weighed an idea in his mind. "If what Gamekeeper says is true," he said finally, "and this geothermal cave network is serving as his headquarters, well, if that is indeed the case, we still have explosives. We can try to seal the entrances or, maybe, if we're lucky, even bring the whole thing down."

Mack scrutinized the poorly lit floor, searching for the charges he had lost during his violent encounter with the new Gamekeeper. As he groped around on the smooth surface, an initial look of hope was briskly followed by one of utter dejection.

Standing up slowly, Mack held up the still intact jumble of explosives in his left hand and displayed a tangled array of cracked plastic housings with severed wires. "Plastique is fine," he muttered. "Detonators are trashed. Big fella must have stepped on 'em. I have no way to set the charges off. Not good." Studying the crumbled components in his hands, he let out an audible sigh as his mind raced to come up with another viable option.

"Come with...me," said a halting, gravelly voice from behind them both. The man-thing motioned to Mack and Josephine with a wave of his beastly arm.

"Gamekeeper stop Matron and bad man," the gigantic creature continued. "I know...where is."

The two allies looked at each other. Up until now, the being formerly known as Bram de Jaeger and now referred to as Gamekeeper had said so little. In fact, Mack had wondered just how much the alien-looking creature truly understood about what was happening around it and if his modified physiology had left him with the ability to engage in higher-order thinking and conversation.

"I will take you," continued Gamekeeper.

"Whoa, fella," cautioned Mack. "I'm about pooped. Tusslin' with you took the last bit out of me. You didn't do my busted rib any favors and I need a rest."

"No!" interrupted Gamekeeper. "Go now!"

With a rough, clawed right hand, the monster-man motioned to and then proceeded to usher in a group of amazing griffin-like creatures. Their long taloned arms and fierce beaked mouths were striking. The air rushed around them as they beat their lumbering, feathered wings up and down in an excited display.

"You rest...we ride," commanded Gamekeeper and he reached out his hand gently and stroked the feathered neck of the vigorous beast next to him.

Fox and Mack both looked at each other with a mix of awe and disbelief.

"Your designs, Doc?" asked Mack with his customary bluntness.

"No, Mack," replied Fox. "Gamekeeper seems to have come up with these on his own."

With that, the hunter and the scientist turned towards Gamekeeper once again as he urged them to come forward and mount the chimeric steeds.

"Quickly...she is...changing and preparing for the reemergence. Hurry!" urged Gamekeeper as they cautiously approached the winged animals. "No time...hurry!"

"What is he talking about?" said Mack as he positioned himself to swing a leg over the now prostrate griffin-thing. "Who is changing?"

Fox had already mounted her designated transport and shook her head. "I can't be certain," she replied. "Matron and Gamekeeper have a unique relationship. From what I can surmise, they are still linked by their shared time with each other. Matron seems to have the initiative and all the answers, but sometimes Gamekeeper catches glimpses or little pieces of the master plan. He looks really agitated. I suggest we go."

Gamekeeper and his winged beast had already moved out from the storage area and through a series of metal doors. As he passed through the last of the monumental edifices, he motioned one last time to them and let out a long guttural cry. Then suddenly, like a bullet released out of a rifle, the mounted monster and his steed burst into a flurry of motion. In an instant, the winged transgenic was airborne and circling above the heads of Mack and Josephine.

"I've been thinking," wondered Mack aloud as he watched the soaring spectacle above him. "How do we know we can trust this Gamekeeper? I mean, wasn't he trying to kill us a few hours ago?"

A slightly dismayed look came over Fox's face as she turned to respond to the hunter. "That wasn't Gamekeeper," she shot back. "That was a hijacked version of Gamekeeper. That was Matron. No, we can trust him."

Mack still looked uncertain. "What makes you so confident?"

"Gamekeeper trusts me," she said with an air of certainty. "He told me so...and he...," Josephine paused for a moment, seemingly unsure if she wanted to divulge any more information to Mack. "He called me, 'The Maiden'," she acknowledged, not sure if that was an appropriate thing to divulge. "Tanaka said something similar to me not long after we first met."

"The Maiden?" questioned Mack. His thoughts were interrupted as the massive set of ebony wings beneath him began to flap frenetically. In an instant, both he and Fox were airborne, flying side-by-side in the cool, rushing air. Looking down, Mack could see what remained of the Birthing House. Up ahead, he saw the jagged, jutting mountainous spire that was the plateau region. It rose to near dizzying heights and stuck out amongst the remainder of the Mega-Preserve's jungle lowlands and savanna. It was staggering and forbidding in appearance. Mack could only imagine what sort of nightmarish horrors they would encounter there.

As the fantastical creatures soared on, Mack scanned the remainder of the jungle beneath him. He soon saw the smoked-out remains of the hunting lodge in which he and Vladimir had taken shelter. A trail of flickering fires, looming smoke, and ash could still be seen around the perimeter of the decimated building.

Vladimir. The crazy Russian had refused to listen to him. He could only think of killing Dominguez since he had learned of his involvement in Vasilli's death. The man had heart, but he arguably let his emotions get the best of him. Now he was dead, killed by Dominguez's transgenic animals. They had been through a lot together. Mack had disliked the Russian upon first meeting him, but he did save his life back at the river. In spite of his criminal nature, Mack had developed a degree of respect for the man which he bestowed on few people. He would miss him.

Suddenly, the flying steeds dove down in a near freefall. Mack grasped the feather-like fur on his mount as the two beasts rapidly followed Gamekeeper's lead.

Down they went, faster and faster. The flying monstrosities appeared to be masters of their aerial domain. As they swooped and dove towards the ground, they did so effortlessly and exhibited a level of grace and sophistication which seemed far beyond what should be possible. The idea that such fantastic beasts had been independently conceived of, designed, birthed, and nurtured by a displaced computer program, that had somehow taken up residence in a dead man's body, still bothered him. The level of design and sheer complexity of these formerly mythological creatures ought to have taken years of planning and testing, yet here he was, aloft upon the impossible.

Within seconds, the trio of flying animals landed with a surprising grace which would have seemed inconceivable anywhere else but in this unearthly place. As Mack dismounted, he noticed that Gamekeeper and Fox had already begun to move closer towards the base of the plateau. The odd couple walked closely, and Gamekeeper's head was cocked to one side as he appeared to be speaking and listening to Fox. The warmth displayed between the two caused Mack to feel a bit cold. "The Maiden" or not, Mack still found their relationship weird and unnerving. Why and how Tanaka had also used such a term sent his mind into full speculation mode.

As they continued on, they were soon joined by a whole host of different transgenic creatures, both large and small. The odd menagerie of animals made no sounds and dutifully filed into line like a well-disciplined battalion of soldiers. Within a matter of minutes, the entire group swelled to well over 100 different animals.

Mack marveled at the creatures' orderliness. At some point, these transgenics had ceased simply being highly modified game species. No, there was almost a sentience about the way they moved and behaved. Somehow, Gamekeeper was able to control these creatures with a degree of regimentation that he would never have deemed possible. What's more, the transgenics converging together did not seem drugged or stuporous. They were lively, alert, and focused. It was as if they somehow understood the stakes involved in what had all the makings of a desperate last stand.

As Mack caught up to his two companions, the sheer size of the plateau began to fully register. The base of the structure looked like it was several miles wide and the mesa-like top was at least several hundred meters tall. There was nothing like it at all in the rest of the Preserve and Mack felt a slight shiver run up and down his spine as he stared at it. He had the sinking feeling that something very sinister was waiting beneath the vast, flat-topped mountain.

"I-inside," cautioned Gamekeeper as he motioned to the base of the plateau. "The Mother...The Bad Mother is inside."

Mack shot a worried look over at Fox. "Bad Mother?" he asked. "What is he talking about?"

Dr. Fox said nothing at first. Apprehension had gripped her face since they arrived. Fox's typical expression was one of trepidation and caution, but this was different. A visage of genuine concern had taken hold.

"Like he said, things are happening rapidly," said Dr. Fox. "Gamekeeper thinks that whatever is inside has evolved into something new and more dangerous."

"More dangerous?" responded Mack.

Fox did not have a chance to say anything. As the group moved to within fifty feet of the large entrance to an expansive cave network, they suddenly found themselves surrounded by legions of snarling transgenics. The horde of creatures howled and screamed, and they began to run and encircle the encroaching invaders.

"Oh, no," muttered Mack. "Look at those nasty things."

Fear forcefully gripped Dr. Fox's face. She was both mad and terrified as she looked up at Gamekeeper.

"Those things look...demonic," continued Mack, not waiting for a reply, "straight up from the pits of hell."

Fox could not argue with that point. The crowd of evil-looking beasts appeared vastly different from those that comprised Gamekeeper's entourage. From the largest pachyderm to the smallest rodent-like species, each member of the roving animal mob appeared bloodthirsty and enraged. All of the creatures sported unnatural looking plate armor which was adorned with grotesque knobs, spikes, and whorls. Yellowish-gray saliva dripped from the horrifying collection of snapping jaws and the taut musculature seemed unnaturally defined, even by transgenic standards. This was a hell-borne army, one bred for conquest and decimation.

"What's your new buddy's plan?" sputtered Mack as he motioned to Gamekeeper. For his part, he demonstrated no signs of fear. He scanned his surroundings carefully, taking in the hellish-animal minions that confronted him with a calmness Mack greatly admired given the circumstances.

"We don't have much time," cautioned Fox. "Gamekeeper will try to hold these enemy transgenics off. He wants us to go inside and stop her."

"'Her'? Who is this 'her'? The 'Bad Mother'?" shot back Mack. "What about weapons to fight Domingo and his beasts? I am a one trick pony and that trick usually requires big guns."

"Like I said, Dominguez is only a tool. He is not really in control and only serves her," said Fox with a forlorn voice. "As for weapons, Gamekeeper told me that the hunter must confront the Bad Mother. He told me that you possess the only weapons that she truly fears."

"Whoa now!" exclaimed Mack noticeably upset. "What are we talking about here? You are The Maiden, Dominguez is trying his level best to kill us, but not really runnin' things, and 'she' is in 'control' of the Preserve? C'mon, Doc. At some point you need to cut out the nonsense and level with me here. I am totally unarmed and this has all the makings of a suicide mission."

Fox said nothing, took several quick steps towards the cave entrance, and cautiously glanced back. The evil-looking transgenics had begun to make their way forward with an ever increasing sense of menace. Several of the larger species let out loud, blood-curdling screams as the group marched forward.

"She's here," stated Dr. Fox. "She was gone for a long time, but she is right here now. She is the one who is responsible for all this death and pain. We must stop her!"

"Oh, for Pete's sake, Doc," yelled Mack. "You've got to pull it together. We have to all be on the same page if we're going to get this done. What are you talking about?"

Dr. Fox quickened her pace and Mack found himself running to keep up. Suddenly, without warning, Gamekeeper reared up and let out a terrifying scream. His formerly calm demeanor had completely melted away, while his body appeared to grow several feet taller, and a rapidly emergent suit of boney, chitinous-like armor formed along his arms and legs. As he signaled to his animal allies, the assembled transgenics furiously let out a series of horrifying howls and viscous wails. The next moment, the entire scene erupted into violence.

Malignant pachyderm-like monsters collided with one another. The various carnivore species exploded into a blur of bloody mayhem. The winged-creatures all took to the air in an exotic display of finely tuned killing. It was as if the transgenic kingdom had lost its collective mind and every creature in the immediate vicinity was programmed with nothing other than the utter death and extermination of its closest animal opponent.

Gamekeeper, for his part, became a terrifying engine of destruction. He ran rough-shod over the newly-minted bestial battlefield with reckless abandon. As he did, he rained down blows from his powerful fists, rent flesh, fur, and bone with his razor sharp claws, and bit mercilessly with his jagged tusk-like teeth. He was indeed a force of nature, a whirlwind of annihilation. His violent display made Mack understand that Gamekeeper had, in fact, been taking it easy on him back at the Birthing House. It was now obvious to him that if he had wanted to, the wild creature could have killed him instantly.

"He will hold them off," assured Dr. Fox as they continued to run towards the mouth of the cave. Within seconds, they entered the rocky entrance to a row of tunnels. As they continued forward, they were met by no further resistance.

An ever increasing heat and foul odor continued to assail them as they walked farther and farther along the rock strewn cave floor. A pulsing sound soon met their ears. It was like a loud base drum beating at a low, sustained rhythm, and the sides of the stone cave walls seemed to almost heave up and down with the eerie reverberations.

"What on earth is that?" asked Mack cautiously as they slowly made their way forward.

"It's her, Mack," replied Dr. Fox. "It's what I was warning you about. The Bad Mother is set to reemerge here."

Mack said nothing as he shuddered with utter amazement. The scene before him said what a thousand words could not.

"It's t-true," stammered Dr. Josephine Fox as she peered ahead in disbelief. "The Mother of Monsters was always controlling the Mega-Preserve."

Chapter 15: The Mother of All Monsters

"She will have your minds and, when she is
finished, she will consume your bodies.
Your sacrifices will further fuel her and
make the coming world a reality."

Mack was about to reply to the scientist next to him when he first caught a glimpse of the globular creature. A muted, white tentacle like-appendage flashed across the far opening of the cave. Mack strained his eyes as he peered down the long passageway again. Upon taking a few steps closer, Mack saw another alabaster whip-like appendage flash across the opening. This time, it was followed by numerous beating arms.

"Mother of Monsters, eh," Mack stated with a forced matter-of-fact tone. "The Father of Freaks must be in the next cave over."

Mack's attempt at levity betrayed a growing sense of unease. He could tell his heart was beating fast and a tight globus sensation had seized hold of his throat. He was scared of what he just witnessed. The wounds he had incurred during his near-death experience with the octopoid transgenic were still fresh on his skin and in his mind. The thing at the end of the stone passage looked to be orders of magnitude bigger, much more complex, and just as mean.

"Do we have a plan, Doc?" said Mack cautiously. "Or do we simply plan on asking M.O.M. here if she'd kindly cease and desist?"

"Gamekeeper has a plan and you have the weapons to fight her," she replied as they continued on.

"Hmmm," muttered Mack with an air of annoyance. "I don't know the plan and I'm completely unarmed aside from a wicked case of body odor. I think this is all crazy, don't you?" scoffed Mack incredulously.

"No," the scientist said simply in response.

Mack shook his head as he followed Fox. The plan was no plan at all as far as he could tell. Tactically, this all made no sense. If you wanted to hunt an animal, you had to at least know something about the animal you were hunting. *Where did it live? What did it eat? When was it active?* Right now, all Mack could be certain about was that whatever this Mother of Monsters was, it stunk to high heaven and he wasn't certain that anything short of a cruise missile could kill it.

Just as Mack and Fox approached the dimly lit opening, a set of the lashing, ivory white, tentacles abruptly shot towards the two amateur spelunkers. Before either could truly grasp what was happening, both Fox and Mack were enveloped by the horrid tendrils and then propelled out of the tight cavern like a pair of slingshot stones.

As the narrow cave gave way to the wide open chamber, the duo let out a collective gasp of horror. The two adventurers had seen and done much in the last few days, but nothing in either of their cumulative experiences had really prepared them for what they now saw before them.

A mass of intertwined tentacled appendages swayed and moved like a patch of gigantic, demonic sea grass. The voluminous arms were a deep white color. Inside the pale extremities was housed an intricate network of vessels, crisscrossing into a chaotic crimson mesh. Following the whipping arms down to their base, Mack could see a collection of pod-shaped masses that seemed to glow with the same indwelling, blood-red series of vessels. All along the floor of the immense chamber, there were winding root-like structures that gave the impression of delving directly into the stone surface. Each floor-imbedded appendage heaved up and down at regular intervals, as if it were attempting to siphon off some substance from its immediate subterranean environment.

Mack and Dr. Fox sped towards the creature until they were within mere feet of one of its suspended elliptical structures. In an instant, the pod of material began to carefully peel open. As it did, a familiar, yet alien face met their eyes.

"Dominguez?" blurted out Mack. "What's going on?"

"Dominguez" said nothing as he stepped forward from his organic cell. Once out, his form was fully exposed to the pulsing light of the geothermals. Like the transformed Bram De Jaeger, the newly-revealed creature before them seemed oddly familiar, yet utterly foreign as well.

The being standing in front of them was nearly eight feet tall, heavily-muscled, and bore thorny talons on his feet and hands. His eyes were a yellow-green and seemed to give off a malevolent glow. His face was long and his lips appeared as taut red lines. He was covered in a prodigious amount of sleek, white fur and he possessed a large swaying tail equipped with a menacing set of prodigious, spiked barbs.

"Oh no. What have you gotten us all into?" exclaimed Mack as his eyes drank in the horror Dominguez had become. The overall shape and modification of his body was similar yet even more monstrous than that into which De Jaeger had been transformed. While Gamekeeper was hideous and entirely unnatural in appearance, there was something altogether different about the changes that had taken place in Dominguez. These particular modifications somehow radiated a sense of the unholy and were undeniably frightfully demonic. Mack could not put his finger on it exactly, but whatever had changed the man before him, one thing was certain: it was pure, unmitigated evil.

"She has been waiting for you both," the inhuman thing said in response. "She will have your minds and, when she is finished, she will consume your bodies. Your sacrifices will further fuel her and make the coming world a reality."

"Let's just skip that and say we did, ugly!" retorted Mack angrily.

The corners of Dominguez's mouth began to draw back in preparation to deliver one of his trademark toothy smiles. As it widened, he displayed a feral-looking set of dentition, far in excess of the formerly gaudy gold-toothed display he had sported not long ago. There could be no doubt that the criminal had made some sort of arrangement with this terrifying creature, this Mother of Monsters. It was as if he had literally sold his soul to her in exchange for his now macabre visage. Mack felt an intense repulsion at the sight of the man-thing.

Setting his steely gaze directly on the trapped hunter, he began to laugh and pointed at the towering white mass with a taloned finger. "Do you see your son and the stupid Russian?" he asked in a haughty tone. "Each has felt the warm embrace of the Mother. Look closely, do you see them?"

Mack looked at the wide base of the gruesome mass. As he did, he quickly noted two suspended elliptical shapes. Held within each circular form was the figure of an adult man. The entrapped men were stone-still and unable to move a muscle. A bundle of pulsing reddish-white tubes had invaded the skin next to the base of the neck. In spite of the milky-white fluid that enveloped and separated them, there could be no doubt as to the identities of the two trapped figures: Michael and Vladimir.

"Noooo!" roared Mack. Tears began to gather in his eyes and his face felt red hot. A spasm of resistance moved through his body, only to be met with a tightening of the encircling arms around him. "You listen to me, Domingo!" he screamed, despite the squeezing organic ligatures. "This isn't over. This isn't over by a long shot!"

The monstrous Dominguez shook his head and eerily smiled as the creature continued to retrieve its prey. "Do not resist her, O'Boyle. It will only prolong your suffering. You have killed many of her children and she has a score to settle." With that, the massive man-creature began to laugh maniacally.

Dr. Fox shot a terrified glance over at Mack as she neared to within inches of an emerging soft-tissue doorway along the side of the creature's quivering alabaster wall of organic material. "No! Nooo!" she screamed as her arms and legs were swiftly enveloped in the tacky mass of tissue. "Help me!" she cried out as the white gelatinous material enveloped her, partially stifling her screams.

"I'm sorry! I don't know what to do!" yelled Mack as the geneticist was pulled fully into the material and completely silenced.

"You are fueling her growth and expanding her consciousness," revealed Dominguez as he passively watched the horrible scene unfold. "The Great Matron is in control now. It won't be long and the whole world will call her Queen once more."

As he listened to Dominguez's demented ravings, Mack watched an identical x-shaped opening form next to the now motionless Dr. Fox who now appeared suspended like a fly in amber. The encircling tentacles from the white beast lurched forward, pulling Mack towards the gelatinous mass. Mack soon felt his face and upper chest enmeshed by the viscous material. A collection of reddish tubes emerged from the whiteout-like background. They probed around the sides of Mack's neck, like a couple of famished lampreys looking for a nutritious place to feed. Once they made contact with his skin, a flood of images took shape in his mind. He could sense an intense, ancient evil well up inside of him. A recurring series of terrifying visions began to appear. Horrible monsters seemed to spring out at him, creatures that were vastly more sinister than any Mack had ever encountered in his life. The parade of beasts - a veritable legion of hell-borne creatures - was then replaced by a pair of sharp, glowing red eyes that materialized in front of Mack. The malevolent orbs belonged to a woman with a surprisingly beautiful face. She possessed a knowing, evil smile and her long white arms began to beckon to the old hunter, as if she were offering him passage to her dark place of origin.

God in Heaven! Mack internally cried out. *Please help me! I know I have done questionable things in my life, but this is not right. I do not want to go out like this!*

As Mack's neck and shoulders were pressed deeper and deeper into the amorphous material, the striking woman's confident smile was replaced by a look of utter repulsion. She fell away from Mack's mind's eye as if she were being cast back into the primordial black pit from which she had crawled out of so long ago. An earth shattering scream clamorously exploded from her lips and she shot a murderous glance at the trapped hunter. Within seconds, the dark lady had disappeared from Mack's thoughts altogether and he found himself once again enmeshed in a tangle of tentacles and bulky viscous material.

While Mack struggled to regain his bearings, an agitated convulsion surprisingly overtook the monster's voluminous form. It was as if every physiologic mechanism contained within the gigantic horror had suddenly been switched off. A mess of white tentacles frantically grasped and pulled at Mack's free legs in an urgent effort to expel his partially-enveloped body.

As this happened, Mack felt his dulled consciousness begin to fully reassert itself. Looking down, he could see his shirt had been ripped open, and there, suspended in a sea of white protoplasm, were his scapular and his St. Hubertus medal. Unlike the rest of the organic and nonorganic objects completely subsumed within the disgusting jelly-like structure, the two metallic objects made the surrounding liquid tissues fold away in a hasty fashion, like an army of cockroaches scurrying away from a single, solitary light source.

Before Mack understood what was happening, he felt his body being thrust backwards and down out of his organic holding cell. A substantial cleave had formed around Mack's scapular and medal, and this opening had extended to encompass him. As he fell, Mack reached out and grasped the Saint's medal and his scapular, pulling them both in close to his weary body. In an instant, he found himself on the hard, rocky floor of the cave, drenched in protoplasmic slime, but completely freed from the interior of the Mother's monstrous form.

Looking up, Mack could immediately tell his former prison was now compromised as the huge structure looked stunned and unable to function as it once had. It was as if contact with Mack's sacramentals had left it in an inoperable state. Mack's thankful mind raced in an effort to surmise just what had happened. *Was it Divine Intervention? Was the dark creature somehow allergic to pewter?* Mack couldn't be sure, but he had somehow been delivered from what seemed like an all but sealed fate just moments ago.

"Thank you, Jesus!" exclaimed Mack as he looked over at the slowed mass. Like a wounded game animal, the tentacled creature appeared incensed, yet debilitated. It had shrunken several orders of magnitude in size and the suspended forms of Mack's son and companions fell to mere feet above the stony cave floor. The pod-like structures containing the still bodies remained tethered to the monster's super structure, but had been ejected outward and clearly remained outside the heavily-walled "skin" of the otherworldly creation.

"Michael!" yelled Mack as he gathered himself from the cave floor and struggled to make his way towards his son's entrapped form. The lone figure inside made no purposeful movement and Mack feared the very worst. As he reached out to Michael, the material encasing his motionless form began to ebb and flow away, like candle wax exposed to hot flame. Within moments, over half of his body was exposed. Mack observed that the white material fled from the jangling metal in his hand. As he reached into the gelatinous mass to cradle his son's seemingly lifeless frame, the last vestiges of his liquid prison fell away with an audible splashing sound.

"Michael! Michael!" Mack repeated as he gently shook his son by the shoulders. "Can you hear me?" For many long moments, the young man was unresponsive. He did not make any respiratory effort and his father could detect no pulse.

Mack shook his son once again in a final desperate attempt to reach him. *Was Michael dead? Should he begin CPR? What had happened to the others? Were they still alive?*

Then, without warning, the lifeless form in Mack's arms suddenly sputtered to life. After several seconds of coughing and vomiting white amniotic-appearing fluid, the young hunter opened his eyes. "I-I just had the worst dream of my life," he mumbled to no one in particular as he stared down at the cave floor in a continued stupor. "Feels like I've been to hell and...back."

"You just might have, Mick," replied Mack as he sympathized with his recovering son. "C'mon...we have to help the others."

Mack supported his weakened son beneath the shoulder and the two made their way directly towards the pod-encased bodies of Dr. Fox and Vladimir Radovich. Their nearly lifeless forms were unmoving, just as Michael's had been a few moments prior.

As Michael bent down to inspect Fox's encased shape, he was struck by the sheer look of terror on her face. Red tendrils extended from her neck towards a long umbilical-like tether. This long red and white tube material was heavily affixed to the main body of the injured Mother. Less than twenty feet away, Vladimir was noted to be in an almost identical situation.

Yet again, Mack was able to easily disassemble the gob of organic material by simply presenting his scapular and his St. Hubertus medal near the egg-like structure. As had happened with Michael, the whitish material simply shed itself away from the unresponsive scientist. Within moments, the young woman began to sputter and choke. She moaned slightly and slowly opened her eyes.

"W-what happened?" she managed to mumble as Mack and Michael looked on. Josephine appeared surprisingly awake, as if a portion of her vitality had been restored and revitalized during her relatively brief confinement in the beast. Her color had improved, and her formerly petite frame seemed somehow more robust, even taller than it was before. The effect was not lost on her companions.

"Concealed weapon," said Mack hastily, not really sure himself what had just occurred. "I don't think it's a stretch to say this 'Mother' is straight up from hell. You gotta get up and we need to fetch Vlad ASAP. That thing is stunned, but I think she'll be back for round two in no time. I don't see Dominguez, but he has to be around here somewhere."

While Michael helped the young woman to her feet, the group looked over at Vladimir's still encased form. Mack stared angrily at the mass of white tentacles a few dozen feet away and yelled to the group to hurry. "C'mon," he said hastily, "We need to roll."

For Michael, time seemed to have slowed meaningfully. His reaction time had increased exponentially and he felt tired and out of it. As the group neared Vladimir, Mack shouted once again. "Oh no, we've got company, people!"

There, before them was Dominguez in his new beastly form, flanked by hundreds of his wild-eyed transgenic minions. Suspended from his right hand was the now motionless and battered form of the man once known as Bram de Jaeger.

"You have hurt our Mother!" hissed Dominguez as he effortlessly tossed the gigantic body of Gamekeeper before the three companions. "What did you do to her?" With that, there was a loud cry of hideous bellows and screams from his assorted beasts. The entire group began to lunge forward angrily.

"Can't say I'm sorry to see the old gal on the ropes," yelled Mack defiantly. "Looks like she bit off more than she could chew, eh?"

Dominguez fumed and his eyes narrowed. He raised his knife-edged clawed hand high above his head, thereby bringing the transgenic engine of destruction to steadily bear down on the small group.

"What do we do?" screamed Fox as she grabbed Michael's hand tightly.

Before Mack could respond, a faint rumbling began to shake and reverberate off the rocky cave walls. All throughout the interior of the cavern, the shaking continued until it was at a near crescendo. In an instant, massive rodent-like creatures emerged from a multitude of deep holes. They quickly scrambled back and forth across the wide expanse with a sense of urgency. A moment later, the formerly subterranean collective disappeared after scattering across the rocky floor and diving into the hard earth.

"Grab Vladimir and the big fella," said Mack as he motioned towards the Russian and Gamekeeper. "I think this was Gamekeeper's plan all along. He just needed enough time for his buddies to do their thing."

"Do their thing?" said Dr. Fox as she caught a glimpse at Dominguez's now disorganized forces. Their cohesion had been disrupted and their ranks splintered. As the series of ever increasing cave-ins continuously pelted their adversaries with rocks and debris, the focus transitioned from one of vicious attack to simple survival.

"C'mon," yelled Mack. "It's gonna all come crashing down!"

As Michael struggled to open Vladimir's pod, it unfortunately became evident that the gangster's long time inside the organic prison had not done him any favors. His body was a pale shadow of its former self. Where once the Russian had been tall and very imposing, the poor creature contained within the structure before them was anything but dangerous appearing. Radovich's now cachectic form looked critically undernourished, and his thin arms and legs looked ready to break at any moment.

"Leave him...to me," said a familiar voice. "You will kill him if you release him now."

It was Gamekeeper. He had suffered some truly grievous wounds and had appeared to be all but dead only moments ago. Several large claw marks decorated his broad chest and a series of nasty bite wounds peppered his shoulders and upper arms. His legs and abdomen were smeared with blood and his left lower leg was bent backwards in an unnatural position.

Mack's mind raced back to their encounter in the Birthing House. He had somehow been able to stab the huge humanoid in the chest, yet the man-thing ultimately shrugged it off as if nothing had happened. *Did he possess some sort of accelerated healing? Was it inherent in other Mega-Preserve creatures?*

Dust and smoke had begun to fill the huge cavern, and Mack frantically scanned the now obscured cave walls for a means of escape. Suddenly, a vigorous pachyderm-like transgenic creature emerged from the crisscrossing chaos of animal movement all around them. It was identical to the animal Mack had encountered inside the huge tanks within the Birthing House, only it was larger and hairier. The hardy creature padded right alongside of Gamekeeper as the beast-man threw out a clawed hand and severed the tendril connecting Vladimir's encapsulated form to the hideous Mother of Monsters. The lacerated, milk-white appendage quickly retreated back towards the pulsating white base. Satisfied that the pod was free, he then hoisted the white container onto the wide back of the waiting hairy transgenic. With the elongated orb secure, the beast of burden burst forward and down a long passageway, presumably leading out of the cavern.

"She must be s-stopped," said Gamekeeper in a low, barely audible voice as he turned to address the remaining group. "S-she has terrible plans for the world."

"Bram," cried Josephine Fox as she gazed up into the sad, yellow eyes of the Gamekeeper. "Are you still there?"

The massive figure bent down and touched the side of the scientist's face. His huge paw, capable of such violence and mayhem, cradled Dr. Fox's cheek in a gentle, almost loving way.

"Protect children," the feral humanoid whispered to the scientist. "Keep them safe. Fight evil outside and inside

Preserve. Dark days ahead." He withdrew his hand and added, "They will take you to safety," diverting his sad eyes from the young woman and looking cautiously at three approaching transgenic pachyderm species. Gamekeeper stared at each creature for only a second and then turned to the group to speak again. "I must make sure you not followed. I must keep it from reaching outside."

With that, Gamekeeper stepped away and scanned the chaotic scene. His eyes briskly locked onto Dominguez's location and, without another word, he confidently burst into a frenzy of motion. Although he was obviously injured, he gave no heed and barreled forward like a heat-seeking missile.

Dominguez had been battling with several strong enemy transgenics. As he dispatched the final one, he stood up, recognized the incoming threat, and likewise exploded headlong into action. In a matter of seconds, the two bipedal monsters were within mere feet of each other and were poised to collide like two opposing forces of nature.

Once they made contact, the two wild brutes immediately became locked in a death struggle the likes of which Mack had never witnessed. Like two mad titans, the angry animal men wrestled, clawed, and bit at each other in a display of violence that far exceeded anything Mack or his son had ever seen in the wild.

"He bought us time, people!" yelled Mack to his group. "He knows what he's doing. Now come on and don't let his sacrifice go to waste!"

With that, Michael grabbed the petite woman and threw her over the back of the nearest waiting beast. He then pulled himself aloft of the same animal and Mack followed suit. In an instant, the robust, heavy-skinned animals took off at a breakneck speed and followed along the same winding series of caves through which Vladimir had been ferried. "This place is coming down any minute!"

Mack strained to look over his shoulder while holding tightly to his transgenic escort. Looking back, he could see a steadily increasing torrent of sharp rocks and magmafied material pelt the unholy abomination. Large furrows and gashes erupted across her amorphous body as the burning petrous missiles continued their haphazard assault unabated. The Mother's whip-like appendages nearly ceased their once non-stop motion and appeared semi-lifeless. Deep open gashes and scorched areas emerged along the exterior of the monster's skin and rivers of evil protoplasmic liquid spilled and mixed with the superheated material along the geothermal vents. A putrid smell far in excess of the initial one encountered in the cave soon overwhelmed the would-be escapees.

"Wow," said Michael still clinging tightly to both his mount and Fox, "I thought that thing stunk when you pulled me out."

"Good chance that's what hell smells like," replied Mack as the threesome dove deeper into the caves.

Suddenly, an echoing shudder went through the whole structure. Splintering cracks began to form along the walls of the side caverns and a tremendous crashing sound nearly pushed the riders from their mounts.

With a series of excited screams, both Michael and Mack urged their transgenic beasts of burden forward. The passage beneath them had become increasingly unstable, and the walls were encroaching tighter and tighter. An expanding plume of hot gasses nipped and bit at the group from behind and beads of sweat broke out on the travelers' foreheads.

Mack and Fox coughed hard as the superheated air mixed with their lungs. It was also becoming more difficult to see. Michael gazed up with beleaguered eyes and caught a small glimpse of the distant opening of the cave. He urged his beast onward, but without warning he felt the massive animal's body give way and shudder to a stop on the ground.

"It's dead!" yelled Michael as he hastily slid down off the back of the pachyderm. "We need to go on foot," he said as they watched the galloping silhouette of his father disappear down the final 100 feet.

All around, the cave continued to shudder and crack. Acrid smoke and dust started to billow as the two young people struggled to make their way forward as best they could. "Josephine," Michael spoke with a real sense of regret in his voice, "we are running out of time. I was supposed to get everybody out of this place alive. I've failed."

Josephine Fox looked back at the young man with a forlorn look, but said nothing. Her lower lip began to quiver ever so slightly, but she could form no words. Any traces of hope had all but vanished from her face.

As the heavy stone walls continued to fracture and heave, Michael suddenly grabbed Josephine by the hand and hastily pulled her towards him. "C'mon," he insisted. "If we die, we die trying to get out of here."

A half-smile emerged on the tired woman's face. It was a look of resolve and admiration. "You're right. I'm with you," was all she said as they plunged headlong down the rocky enclosure.

Michael held onto Josephine's hand tightly as they attempted to run out of the cave. Making their way towards what Michael thought was the way out, his thoughts traveled back to the first time he met Dr. Fox. She was present the day of his interview with De Jaeger and had said very little during the meeting. He easily recalled how she had stared at him with those cold, analytical eyes. She took voluminous notes throughout their time together and Michael had never forgotten the weirdness of it all. It had been as if he was another anomaly in need of analysis and taxonomy. Her blunted emotional spectrum struck him as bizarre.

Although the two of them had worked together for several months, Michael still knew very little about the woman and was continually struck by her very business-like, almost detached demeanor. She kept mostly to herself and had revealed very little about her background. Any attempts by Michael to strike up conversation with her were met with awkward silence or one word answers. Ultimately, Michael had decided that Fox simply found him boorish and not worth her time.

The enigma that was Josephine Fox was not yet solved. If anything, it had only deepened. Michael still remained uncertain as to just what exactly Josephine's role may or may not have been in all this unfolding madness. After all, the Preserve was her baby and she, more than any other person, was responsible for its existence. That said, they were both now in very real danger of dying. The fact that all of them had been nearly killed several times over convinced him that Fox was telling the truth, or at least what she thought was the truth. She had attempted to control technology that, in spite of her brilliance, was still beyond her abilities to fully command. He truly wondered, *Was her greatest sin one of intellectual pride?*

Several large rock piles had formed around them and the floor was heavily littered with debris from the cave walls and the ceiling. Their path to the outside was becoming more and more congested and they both slowed down substantially as they attempted to address the ever increasing obstacles before them.

Michael scanned all around for signs of light. He strained his eyes to the left and to the right, but could see very little. The cave was becoming increasingly filled with choking dust to the extent that he could barely see structures two feet away. Any means to accurately orient direction had been removed. They were lost and most likely trapped inside the tunnel. *Did the cave still possess a viable opening?* It was impossible to tell and it would not even matter if they did not know what direction to go.

Just as Michael was about to scream out in frustration, a familiar voice rang out, reverberating off the steadily crumbling walls.

"You two look like you could use a ride," said Mack as he leaned over the ponderous beast he sat astride. "Get on!"

"D-dad?" Michael sputtered, not sure if he could trust his ears.

"Yeah, Son," replied the familiar voice. "My new buddy must have sensed his friend had given up the ghost. We were almost outside when Big Boy here spun around and found his way back. Pretty remarkable!"

Mack O'Boyle bent down and patted the transgenic on its hairy neck and the beast let out a contented guttural tone that sounded like a cat's purr mixed with a howler monkey call. As it did, the beast deftly turned 180 degrees and then proceeded to bend low.

"C'mon," urged Mack. "He's fast, but this place is wrecked. We gotta get a move on!"

Clambering on the back of Mack's mount, the group resumed its hasty retreat. The abject darkness suddenly began to lighten when Josephine called out excitedly. "Light ahead!" she screamed. "I can see the opening!"

The hairy pachyderm, seemingly urged on by his passengers' excitement, quickened its already prodigious pace and barreled onward, deftly navigating debris with the surefootedness of a mountain goat. Within seconds, the three people found themselves at the cave's entrance and had just exited the opening when the entire plateau superstructure began to crumble, and a massive crack liberally formed along the mid-portion of the supporting rock edifice above them. This was followed by a terrific splintering sound followed by a number of thunderous pops. Huge boulders began to heavily rain down from the plateau's highest levels. As they did, a large-scale crevasse formed along the base of the rock formation and soon enveloped the monolithic structure. Smoke and gas continued to belch out of the myriad openings to the formerly hidden subterranean realm. Within seconds, the entire rocky superstructure broke into pieces and completely collapsed upon itself, filling the newly-formed chasm and leaving only a dusty, rock strewn crater in the earth.

"We're alive!" affirmed Mack as he surveyed the devastation before him and looked over fondly at Michael and Josephine. "Thank God!"

Mack embraced his son and Josephine Fox in a collective hug. He'd figured his chances of surviving the Mega-Preserve had been infinitesimally small. His chances of finding his son alive had seemed even less likely. Yet, here he was, alive with his son and the geneticist who had so doubted him.

After several seconds, Mack looked up and stared at the now decimated plateau. *Was the Mother of Monsters dead? What about the monstrously altered Dominguez? Could Gamekeeper have survived the violent cave-in?*

Michael studied his father. He had tears in his eyes. They had survived what had seemed to be truly unsurvivable and now they could look to the future, a future that had been anything but certain only a few short minutes ago. "Well," said Michael, "what do we do now?"

Mack looked at Dr. Fox for a moment and then back at Michael. There were still a great many things about the Mega-Preserve that the three of them did not know. Some of the transgenics had survived the cave-in. Many were injured and some were near death. Others, like Mack's new steed, Big Boy, were simply grazing nearby, comfortably oblivious to what had just occurred.

The Mega-Preserve and the creatures inside now represented something far more important than a glorified kill zone for rich hunters. This place had been transformed into a biological wonderland with nearly unlimited opportunity for scientific research. The rich biodiversity and extreme degree of hyper-speciation could keep the scientific community busy for decades.

But in spite of all those things, the Mega-Preserve was also a crime scene. Men had been killed and horrible acts had been committed. Dominguez had somehow tapped into a dark, malevolent force whose exact nature was still uncertain, but whose ultimate intentions were anything but benevolent.

"We have a lot of decisions to make," said Mack finally. "I'm not even sure where to begin." Mack surveyed the imploded plateau area with concern. Hot gasses were still readily billowing from the base of the stone ruins. "What I am certain about is this: this place is fragile and its potential for danger cannot be overstated. We are the only people who really understand what the Preserve represents and the secrets it contains."

Dr. Josephine Fox and Michael nodded their heads in unified agreement.

"I have spent a lifetime hunting and killing transgenics," Mack acknowledged soberly. "Maybe we can save a few this time around."

Chapter 16: Only the Beginning

"The thing you encountered inside the cave system is very old and very evil."

"I say, old boy," professed Alistair as he twiddled the tip of his droopy mustache, "you've done a man's job."

Mack smiled as he viewed his long-time friend from behind the quarantine shielding. It was erected soon after the Preserve was brought back under control and had been a purely precautionary measure initially, but attempts to remove the group were stifled by continued concerns about possible biological contamination.

"Thanks, buddy," replied Mack with a smile. "It's good to see you. I'm looking forward to getting out of here. De Jaeger's people still cannot be sure that their mop-up is 100 percent effective. They have introduced outside food, and so far we have all tolerated it. With that, they tell me we should be able to exit in another month or so."

"I'm sure it feels like an eternity," said Alistair as he dug through his attaché case and produced a rather worn handheld device. "I did bring you the information you requested."

Mack's old friend placed the device on the table before the barrier between them and the screen suddenly came to life. A series of odd symbols and hieroglyphic images began to swim around and hover above the projection.

"I must say," continued Alistair, "I nearly exhausted my list of contacts procuring this. People either laughed at me or became so terrified regarding the subject that it was difficult to obtain any clear details."

"Yeah," said Mack, "I figured as much. Anyway, what did you find?"

An unmistakable look of trepidation suddenly took over Alistair's face. He opened his mouth to speak, but stopped suddenly.

"C'mon," grumbled Mack, "out with it."

"Well," said the old man, "from what my sources have gathered, I have good reason to think you're correct. The thing you encountered inside the cave system is very old and very evil."

"What else?" Mack inquired.

"I don't think this is the first time mankind has encountered this 'Mother' creature you described. From what I can piece together, an entity matching this description has been interacting with human beings throughout recorded history," explained the Englishman.

"What do you mean?" asked Mack with concern in his voice.

"Well," said Alistair as he swiped his hand across the flat screen. When he did, a new series of horrendous looking monsters with decidedly female characteristics began to take shape. The twisted depictions started out in a static formation and then began to writhe and move in a rhythmic, repetitive display. "Many ancient cultures maintained a deep-seated belief in a dark, supernatural matron that produced diabolical offspring to menace the world. The Greeks referred to this entity as Echidna, the Anglo-Saxons fought against Grendel's mother, the Hebrews believed in a dark female power named Lilith, and the Norse held that an evil being called Angerboda gave rise to a number of deadly beasts."

"You're talking about myths, legends, fairy tales, Al," protested Mack. "What I saw and felt inside that cave was no make-believe story. It was real, and it was in control of everything. It had an intelligence about it that was totally malevolent."

Mack felt a shudder move through his whole being as he recalled his experience inside the deep, dark cave. There could be no doubt, the tentacled nightmare had left an indelible mark on his memory, but it was the woman with the red eyes, the one he encountered inside the massive white creature's main structure, that he could not forget. She had haunted his dreams ever since the incident and Mack found himself thinking about her daily. Although he could not say why or how, Mack was convinced that the creature was still somehow alive.

"Which brings me to another detail about your encounter with this thing," continued Alistair as he peered forward and once again lightly touched the screen between them.

"It has to do with your sacramentals," motioned Alistair as he pointed to Mack's chest. "The Roman Catholic scapular and the St. Hubertus medal you have been wearing for the last few years: what do you know about them?"

Mack reached down into his shirt and produced the two metal objects. As he peered down at them, he immediately noted the details of the St. Hubertus medal. The engraved pewter object depicted a man with a shepherd's crook flanked by a hunting dog and a stag. The stag had a cross between its antlers and the dog was sitting at the foot of the standing man. Mack's scapular was similar in size, only rectangular in shape. In the center was the figure of Jesus Christ with His right hand pointing to His exposed heart. Mack had never taken the time to really look at the scapular or truly study the medal of the patron saint of hunters. As he recalled, a Catholic missionary had insisted that he "enroll" in the scapular and his wife gave him the St. Hubertus medal several years ago.

"A missionary priest in South Africa gave me the scapular awhile back," said Mack finally. "He told me about the Sacred Heart of Jesus and a few other things that I have since forgotten. Seemed like a nice, old guy so I took it to humor him. Mary gave me the St. Hubertus medal just before she got sick. Again, I wore it mostly because it mattered very much to her. She told me it was a third class relic, but I never took the time to really research what that meant. I always figured they were mostly good luck charms. You know I grew up Catholic; however, I haven't been to Mass in a very long time."

Alistair studied his friend of many years. He stared at the extended silver chain around Mack's neck and then studied the two shapes dangling lightly at the end.

"And you're certain that this Mother of Monsters creature was repelled by those objects and nothing else?" asked Alistair with intense interest.

Mack recalled his near-death encounter once again. His memory for his time inside the horrible amorphous blob was dim, but he remembered seeing the evil woman's face and how he felt his life-force slowly begin to bleed away second by second. He also recalled how the moment his scapular and his medal made contact with the evil entity, he immediately felt a loosening of the grip she had on his body. No, there could be no doubt that there was something about his pewter scapular and St. Hubertus medal that had stopped the evil creature from killing him and the others under her control.

"Yeah," said Mack without a trace of hesitation. "This thing was several stories tall, whitish, had tentacles like a squid, displayed oblong pods all along its body, and could house material inside its liquid form. It had us all wrapped up and we believe Dominguez was completely under its control. We were all as good as dead, but the moment my medals made contact with her, she couldn't get away quickly enough."

Alistair touched his screen and presented an image that appeared to be identical to the creature Mack had encountered in the cavern. "Is this what you saw?" asked Mack's friend as he blew up the image slightly.

Mack felt himself physically recoil as his eyes locked onto the tangled horror. He could feel his face become flushed and his heart beat hard in his chest. "W-where did you find that, Al?" was all Mack managed to stammer.

"This particular picture was reproduced from an ancient Sumerian text. After I found it, I did some additional research and located similar pictorial depictions and written descriptions of nearly identical creatures. Duplicate images can be found across Eurasia, Africa, the Americas, and Oceania. The dates vary somewhat, but most seem to have been recorded around 4,000 BC."

"So this thing has been around for over 6,000 years?" asked Mack. "Where did it come from? What is it?"

"I'm not a religious man," prefaced Alistair. "That being said, I am a practical bloke. From what I have gathered from you, my research, and my contacts, I think we can safely say that this creature is older than recorded history and it is most likely...demonic in nature."

A stunned silence filled the space between the two hunters. *Had Mack heard his friend correctly?* "Demonic?" Mack shuddered with a deep dread. To hear his longtime friend say the word sent him back on his heels. Up until now, Mack had genuinely felt that the creature in the cave could not have been anything but hell-born. He had been hesitant to say anything more specific or to probe his fellow survivors until he had a chance to do more research. Alistair's bold confirmation left him speechless and perplexed. He felt oddly affirmed, but also extremely unsettled by the new information and the high likelihood that it could take him to places he had never been and, in all truthfulness, places he was scared to explore.

"I don't fully understand the why or the how, but I can confirm from your first hand experiences that the creature was incapacitated by your third class relic and your scapular. Demonic forces are repelled by holy objects, by sacramentals. I've researched it and that is a fact. It is the only logical explanation."

"Hmmm, can we really be sure about this?" cautioned Mack. "I mean..."

"I'm sure," said a familiar voice over Mack's shoulder. Turning around, Mack watched as Dr. Josephine Fox made her way to the table Mack was seated at. The young woman sat down next to the old hunter and immediately began to study the horrific image before her.

"That is the Mother of all Monsters," said Dr. Fox not averting her gaze from the projected terror displayed before the two men.

"Gamekeeper warned me about her, but even he did not fully understand her nature. When I was trapped inside, she showed me her plan in all its detail. She is the product of the highest demons in hell itself, a being of pure evil who wants to destroy humanity, to literally create hell on Earth. She would cast a shadow over the earth the likes of which has not been seen for thousands of years. She controlled Dominguez, but he was not the only one. She has acolytes across the globe."

Mack and Alistair said nothing for a moment. Josephine had said very little following the final incident in the cave. Mack just figured that the poor woman was shell-shocked and suffering from a well-deserved case of PTSD. He had seen it all happen before, and she fit the profile.

But Fox was saying things and corroborating theories that she would have been hard pressed to even acknowledge a few short days ago. After all, wasn't she supposed to be an empirical scientist and a defacto atheist? She had laughed at Mack during his mere mention of God or a higher power taking any interests in the affairs of man. Now she was describing ancient demonic forces and their perverted goals for the earth with a matter-of-factness that would take some getting used to. No, something had most certainly changed in the good doctor since encountering the Mother of Monsters.

"She's not dead, Mack," added Josephine Fox with a forlorn voice. "Don't ask me how I know that, but I can tell you with 100 percent certainty that she is not dead, and we have not seen the last of her."

As Fox finished speaking, Mack felt a cold chill emerge from the back of his neck and run down the length of his spine. A dark thought had needled its way into his tired mind: *Who was Dr. Josephine Fox?* That is to say: *Who was she really?* He had to admit that he truly did not know much about the woman. She had a well-deserved reputation as a brilliant geneticist, but other than that, she was a complete enigma. About her education, her family, her childhood, Mack had learned only the bare minimum. She said very little and offered up even less. It wasn't that he didn't trust her, but he'd found that he could never feel at ease around her. His intuition told him that she was a woman with a great many secrets, some of which she may not have even been aware of herself.

No other human being on the planet had been more instrumental in the creation and the design of the Mega-Preserve. She was, after all, according to Gamekeeper and Tanaka, The Maiden, and like it or not, her pride and joy had more likely than not produced a malevolently dark creature, the likes of which had been utterly inconceivable to everyone only a short time ago. *Was it somehow true that Gamekeeper had been co-opted by unknown forces and harnessed for someone's sick private agenda, or was the truth far more disturbing?* Fox upheld the belief that Dominguez was nothing more than a proxy which the Mother had taken control of and used. *But was that really true? Was it possible he had known Josephine prior to the hunt? Was there a secret connection between them?*

These intrusive thoughts scared Mack, and he resolved then and there to observe Dr. Fox carefully and make it a point to learn all he could about the mysterious woman. He prayed that he was being overly vigilant, and that, given time, all of these worries and distrust would evaporate, but he still needed answers.

"What are you saying, Doc," said Mack cautiously as he successfully regained his focus. "Do you believe this thing still poses a threat?"

"I think we need to be extremely careful about who is allowed access to the Preserve," she said. "I also think we have to expose the people who are responsible for this. We must locate them and stop them, or they will find a way to bring her back. I will communicate with De Jaeger's people and make sure we have input as to what happens next."

"My dear doctor," challenged Alistair, "what are you suggesting?"

"We're suggesting that we cannot sit by and wait for these people to make another play," said Michael O'Boyle as he entered the room, pushing Vladimir Radovich in a wheelchair. The formerly formidable-appearing Russian gangster appeared thin and sickly. His black beard now had large patches of white in it, and he looked tired and bent as he and Michael approached the group.

For the last few days, he had been recuperating under De Jaeger's physician's supervision with input from Dr. Fox. Immediately after being removed from beneath the plateau, he was evacuated to the Birthing House Complex. A makeshift hospital had been assembled there and a series of medical interventions were performed in an attempt to stabilize him, including IV fluids, antibiotics, and TPN. Also, a complete gene sequencing was performed and his DNA appeared 100% intact. Thankfully, Vladimir was feeling better every day, but he still had weeks of recovery time before him.

"My brother was killed by this Mother of Monsters and those under her control. Dominguez did not act alone," he growled weakly. "I will find them all... every last one." Despite his weakened condition, the Russian's steely resolve was still as evident as ever. A man of lesser convictions would have cut his losses, abandoned any consideration of retribution after nearly dying, and simply focused on recovering. Vladimir had proven himself to be anything but ordinary.

Mack turned around and inspected the gathering group. It was quite a crew. He never dreamed his life's ultimate direction would lead him here, but that is exactly where he found himself. If what these people were saying was even 50 percent correct, he could not ignore it. Their first priority was safeguarding the Preserve. Once that was accomplished, they could get down to the task of learning the real story about what had happened inside this place and just who was truly responsible. At some point – hopefully soon – they could reenter the outside world, but not before other looming issues were resolved.

"Well, Al," said Mack, "it looks like I'm gonna be busy for the foreseeable future. Can you clear my schedule?"

"Already done," replied Alistair without missing a beat. "Oh, and I took the liberty of having all of your equipment transferred here. I suspect you'll need it."

A grin emerged on Mack's weathered face as he listened to Alistair go on about all of the logistical issues he had had to deal with over the past few days. He sounded like an old, squawking mother hen as he went on and on about bribing officials and the multiple roadblocks he contended with in procuring certain contraband items. But it sounded like they might very well need all of those supplies and more. It was very likely the Mega-Preserve could simply be the tip of a very secret, very dangerous iceberg. Mack would have to be careful about whom he trusted and what inquiries he made. Something told him that he had not put his best hunting days behind him. No, he was simply trading in the

241

hunting of transgenic creatures for the hunting of the most elusive thing of all: the Truth.

Epilogue: The Order Revealed

"Yes, Father. I will do what is required of me.
No more, no less."

"Brother Tanaka is dead," said the somber-looking man as he handed a nondescript manila envelope to the seated figure behind a heavy oak desk.

The man, obscured by the dim light of the office, took the envelope, inspected the papers inside briefly, and then proceeded to set them down off to the side of his computer. "How did it happen?" he commented after reviewing the contents.

"I-information is limited, but it appears he was killed while operating inside the environment," replied the younger man visibly saddened over the news.

"So it seems Matsumo was correct about that place. He always had an uncanny intuition," said the man behind the desk. "What about De Jaeger? Do you think he understood what he was helping to create?"

A silence gripped the room. The young man peered down at his feet for several seconds before looking up with a forced sense of resolve. "It is believed that he was ultimately killed, but not before he underwent a substantial...transformation," answered the man now dutifully standing with his hands at his sides. "As to how much he actually knew about the facility's true nature and ultimate purpose, I cannot say. It is entirely possible his father kept many secrets from him. As far as we know, he remained uninitiated."

"I see," said the seated man as he shifted his substantial weight back into the recesses of the big chair. He seemed to be recalling past events with the demeanor of a man who had been in one too many harrowing adventures. "What else?" he said, suddenly looking up.

"Well," continued the young man. "We also believe that one of the other clients was physically altered at some point during the incident inside the Mega-Preserve. That was a most unexpected development and one we are also still researching. It is unknown what, if any, ties he might have had to Lightbringer or the Matrons."

"Did the geneticist survive?" inquired the other man with a concerned tone.

The younger man said nothing for a moment. He seemed uncertain and slightly hesitant. At last he responded, "Y-yes, Josephine Fox is alive. As of right now, we believe she is oblivious as to her true role in all of this. I speculate that Brother Tanaka was able to achieve some limited deprogramming either before or during the hunt. I'm guessing the process is incomplete, but it does help to explain his partial success."

Silence gripped the dark room and the man across the desk looked deeply pensive. "May God have mercy on her soul," he finally managed to say after several tense seconds.

"She is a victim," cautioned the young man. "After many years of observation and bloodline studies, Brother Tanaka felt she was potentially the most dangerous person on the planet. She had all of the tools and training to accomplish their goals."

"Given what she has done thus far, I cannot disagree," said the other man. "I wish now we had taken Matsumo more seriously. He saw this coming for a long time. I am getting old and inflexible in my thinking," he replied shaking his head with a mix of anger and disappointment. "What is the status of the Preserve right now?"

"At this time," returned the young man, "we believe we have things contained. The survivors have all been quarantined within the facility and are available should we need to reach them. Based on our prior experience, it could be several more weeks until they can safely be released from that environment."

"And we have people overseeing that?"

"Yes, Father," the other man quickly replied. "I saw to it as soon as we decided to insert Brother Tanaka into the facility. We now have a team of several men working inside De Jaeger's company. It was relatively easy to gain access after the incident given the total disarray the company found itself in."

"What about her?" the priest continued. "Do you believe she was able to break through?"

"We cannot be certain, Father," stated the young man soberly. "She has once again come very close to full reemergence. That being said, if she had, I don't think we would be having this conversation. My reports are that a large stone structure was imploded in the center of the environment and a Mater Malum organism was most likely killed inside. If that is true, it does set their efforts back, at least temporarily. Recent history has taught our Order that when an attempted reemergence is disrupted, the forces of evil either scrap the entire operation or make every effort to retrieve their Great Matron directly. Retrieval and transference is a much less controlled process and much more dangerous for those involved, but it is also harder for us to directly target and prevent. As you know, very few human beings have ever entered into the Motherlands and returned alive."

"Who else knows anything about this?" the big man shot back.

"Our people in Cape Town and Cairo report that a man named Alistair Winslow has been talking to a great many people regarding very similar topics. He is affiliated with a man famous in elite transgenic hunting circles by the name of Mack O'Boyle. He was actually inside the Mega-Preserve where he managed to recover his son and save several others."

"O'Boyle, you say? That is very interesting," mused the older man seemingly lost in thought for several seconds as a subtle smile crossed his bearded face.

The young man nodded in agreement and said nothing more.

"What do we know about this Mr. O'Boyle?" questioned the priest as he observed the young man intently.

"He's hunted and killed everything that walks on four legs and he has a sterling professional reputation. His formerly estranged wife, Mary O'Boyle, is now deceased. His son is an accomplished hunter in his own right and is also a zoologist and veterinarian by training," the young man reported.

"Does this Mack O'Boyle possess any particular belief system?" wondered the priest. "Do you know if he is a religious man? Can he be trusted?"

"I don't know for certain," the young man weakly acknowledged. "Reports are that he went toe-to-toe with a Mater Malum and survived, thereby preventing the reemergence, almost single-handedly. Not an easy task, especially for someone with no obvious familiarity with the occult or how to formally combat it."

The imposing man behind the heavy desk stood up. He was a tall man – at least 6 foot, 6 inches – and looked as if he weighed well over 300 pounds. As he walked towards the far right side of the room, his white beard gleamed briefly beneath the sparse lighting. Upon reaching the wall, he waved his hand over a flat view screen. A moment later, a small metal drawer emerged from the wall with a low hissing noise. The older man then reached into the enclosure and pulled out a sizable glass vial. Contained inside it was a long, cylindrical piece of alabaster tissue. A line of small suction cups could be seen along the volar surface of the object. A collection of devitalized red vessels coursed along the length of the tissue remnant and formed beveled openings on either side of the severed appendage's ends. Motioning to his young companion, he handed the vial to him.

"The last time I encountered her," he said as he placed the sealed container in his companion's right hand, "she and her monsters almost killed me and nearly took over my soul." The big man mused as his opposite hand went up to trace the path of a deep scar across the length of his face, "That was many, many years ago and if not for God's divine intervention, we would have lost everything.

The old cleric seemed to physically wince at the memory of the Order's near defeat. Maximilian had studied that particular battle a great deal and it was a well know fact that the priest was one of the few remaining survivors from that time. In spite of this, the priest had said very little about what had actually taken place during the conflict. The cost in blood and treasure had been immense and, at one point, even threatened to dissolve the Order.

"As you know," continued the priest, "this Order was created and has been maintained because of their Great Matron's omnipresent threat and because of those misguided individuals who continue to support and serve her. Take that specimen and find this hunter, O'Boyle. Show it to him, and inform him as to the true nature of the struggle into which he finds himself. I sense in him a potentially strong ally. If we are right about the Mega-Preserve, our enemies will have already dispatched their people to Africa. All of the survivors are in grave danger. We don't have much time."

"Yes, I will see to it immediately, Father." With that, the young man turned and hastily made his way to the door. Just as he was about to leave, he heard a voice call out from behind him.

"Wait a moment, Maximilian. There is one other thing."

Maximilian stopped, turned around, and looked back towards the towering priest, "Yes, Father?"

"I want you to have this," he said as he reached into his long black cassock and produced a dramatic black crucifix. Handing the impressive crucifix to the young man, he smiled warmly. "Remember, she is an opponent capable of great cunning and evil. Her essence is demonic, the spawn of the worm himself. Her Familiars are everywhere and it seems that the rules in this conflict are changing in ways we do not yet fully understand. Never forget, you are amongst the most well trained of all the Brothers here, but she will test you as you have never been tested before. Remember your teacher, Brother Tanaka, and never let your guard down. Pray to God and His Holy Blessed Mother for strength and never forget who you are. Do you understand?"

"Y-yes, Father" said Maximilian resignedly, "I understand and I will not fail the Order." With that, the young man turned and exited the room, a steely look of determination writ large on his face.

"Oh, and Maximilian, one more thing," said the priest with a genuinely melancholy tone.

"Yes, Father," he said, turning around to face him.

"If the scientist cannot be contained through non-violent means, you may be forced to perform more drastic measures. Are you prepared to carry out such actions should the need arise?"

Maximilian nodded his head resolutely and replied, "Yes, Father. I will do what is required of me. No more, no less."

With that, the young man turned and made his way from the dark room with quick, but determined steps.

The old priest listened as the sound of the young brother's footsteps disappeared down the hall. Sitting down, he reached into a side desk drawer and opened it. After several seconds of purposeful searching, the man produced a small wooden box from a recessed space inside the drawer. It measured approximately 10 inches square and was emblazoned with a large metallic chi rho symbol.

As he removed the lid, a satisfied look overtook his face and he stared at the box's contents for several seconds. Then, almost without thinking, the big man reached inside and pulled out a silver chain with a semi-lustrous medal on it. Taking the medal into the palm of his hand, the priest inspected it carefully and then placed it back inside the box.

"May the Good Lord and His loyal servant, St. Hubertus, protect us all from what is coming," he said as he once again traced his hand along the length of his scarred face.

The End

"I think we can safely say that this creature
is older than recorded history and it is
most likely...demonic in nature."

About the Authors

Mark and Staci McKeon write from their home in a secluded wooded area of Iowa where they homeschool and unschool their 7 rambunctious children. Mark is a cradle Catholic who reverted to the Faith, and Staci was a radical feminist agnostic who converted and was baptized before they married in 2004. They, with their children, love learning about the Faith and attend the Traditional Latin Mass near their home.

Special thanks to Steve Ott for his terrific artwork and to Brad Miller for helping us format the book. We could not have done this without either of you!

Made in the USA
Las Vegas, NV
12 October 2021

32206771R00148